# Prairie Fire!

## Bill Freeman

James Lorimer & Company, Publishers,
Toronto, 1998

James Lorimer & Company acknowledges the support of the Department of Canadian Heritage and the Ontario Arts Council in the development of writing and publishing in Canada. We acknowledge the support of the Canada Council for the Arts for our publishing program.

Cover illustration: Jeff Domm.

Canadian Cataloguing in Publication Data
Freeman, Bill, 1938—
    Prairie fire!

ISBN 1-55028-609-9 (bound)  ISBN 1-55028-608-0 (pbk.)

I. Title

PS8561.R378P72 1998   jC813'.54   C98-930198-2
PZ7.F64Pr   1998

James Lorimer & Company Ltd., Publishers
35 Britain Street,
Toronto, Ontario
M5A 1R7

Printed and bound in Canada.

*For Erik, Peggy, Jessica and Nathan*

# Foreword

For decades in the nineteenth century the Red River Settlement was governed by the Hudson's Bay Company, and the lives of the people were dominated by the fur trade. This was the preserve of the Métis, a proud and independent people who shared both French and Indian cultures. But in the 1870s things suddenly changed: the Red River settlement became a part of Canada, and the new province of Manitoba was created; the buffalo suddenly disappeared leaving the Métis and the Indians in crisis; and settlers from Ontario began to pour into the province seeking free land, land that the Métis believed was their own.

*Prairie Fire!* is a story about the people of Manitoba who lived in these times. It is a tale of hardship, racial hatred, and love. Above all it is a story of one family who rose above the conflict of their time to create a new life for themselves and the people around them. The story is fiction but the lives of the people it describes and the hardships they faced are part of the real history of the people of Canada.

Bill Freeman

# The Homesteader

*On the distant lonely prairie,*
*In a little lonely shack,*
*New life the homesteader faces;*
*On the world he's turned his back.*

*He's fifteen miles from a neighbour*
*And a hundred miles from a town;*
*There are rolling plains between them;*
*It is there he's settled down.*

*Through day-long hours of bright sunshine,*
*With the twilight into night,*
*Through the fierce hot rays of summer*
*And the autumn's paler light.*

*Through night-long hours of deep darkness*
*And the glare of winter snow,*
*With the roar of well-fed fires,*
*And forty degrees below.*

*Through the plowing and the sowing,*
*When the dust blows black from fields,*
*Then the welcome rains of springtime*
*Bring him dreams of harvest yields.*

*Through the golden glow of harvest,*
*With showers the grain to fill,*
*Through the fear of threatening hail storm*
*And the fierce hot winds that kill.*

*With age-old wisdom behind him,*
*And spurred by his own great need,*
*Thus he builds his broad foundations*
*Free from custom and from creed.*

Jonathan Hughes Arnett

# 1

The Bains family hurried along the muddy Winnipeg street, past the wooden stores and houses that lined the road.

"Come on, Kate," Meg called to her younger sister, who had fallen behind. "We want to be the first in line when the land registry office opens."

Kate was tired from the trip and had slept very little in the tiny hotel room the five members of the family had shared the night before, but she hurried to catch up and walk beside her fourteen-year-old brother, Jamie.

"Now, remember," their mother, Peggy, lectured. "Let me do the talking. This is important. We have to get our land registered properly."

Peggy had that determined look on her face that the other members of the family had learned meant serious business. She walked in front, holding the hand of Robbie, the youngest member of the family. She held up her long dress as she dodged the mud puddles left from the spring rains. Behind came Meg, a sixteen-year-old girl, who still managed to look pretty despite the sober look that matched their mother's expression. And behind her came Jamie and Kate, tired, a little dirty and rumpled, but attentive to the words of their mother.

Peggy's determination came from a conviction that homesteading in Manitoba was the one chance the family had to build a future for itself. It was 1876, and now that the Métis rebellion was over, and the territory was organized into a new province, the vast prairie was open to new settlers who wanted to farm. If they could just get land, the Bains family could build a new life.

Robbie was the only one who seemed genuinely excited about their prospects. He called out the numbers on the street as they passed until he spotted the right building. "There — Dominion Land Office," he read from the lettering painted on the glass door. The family came to an abrupt halt.

It was a few minutes before the land office opened. Peggy had hoped to be the first one in line, but already three men were gathered in front of the glass door. They were small, wiry men with black hair and dark faces. They wore rough homespun suits, felt hats, and heavy boots.

"Métis … " Jamie whispered to Kate. Already he had come to recognize the local people, who were a mixture of Indian and French. He felt a sudden twinge of fear go through him. The boy had heard stories of the uprising led by Louis Riel a few years before. An Orangeman named Thomas Scott had been executed in the rebellion, and Jamie sensed that the Métis disliked and distrusted all English-speaking Canadians.

The three men appeared anxious. Could they be looking for trouble? But before anyone from the family could ask what was going on, a middle-aged man, dressed in a black, sober business suit and a bowler hat came striding down the street and approached the group gathered around the door. "What are you doing here?" the man demanded sharply of the Métis.

"*Ma terre, c'est —*" the oldest of the three Métis started to explain in French, but he was not given a chance.

"I told you when you were here before that you can't take title to the land you want to claim. The Métis were given a million acres out on the prairie. Go and farm there!"

The Métis obviously could not understand what the man was saying to them. *"Mais oui, monsieur. Mais ..."* The rest was lost in a babble of voices Jamie did not understand.

The stern bowler-hatted man fumbled with the keys to the office and then opened the door. He appeared to be the clerk in charge of the land registry office. "I'll tell you one last time. This land is for settlers — English settlers! Now get out of here before I call the magistrate!"

The confusion and concern was clear in the faces of the Métis. They were immobilized by the harsh tone. For the longest time, they stared through the door, unable to speak, watching the clerk ready the office for the day's business. Then there was a stream of French or some other language as they talked between themselves.

"Monsieur, is there something that we can do to help?" Peggy asked the Métis in French.

*"Les Anglais ..."* one of the Métis said and then gave an expression of frustration.

For a moment Jamie thought that they might attack the office and the clerk. It was clear that their anger had pushed them to the brink of rebellion, but the brash arrogance of the clerk had unnerved them.

"What did they say?" Jamie whispered to Kate, whose French was much better than his.

"Something about their land rights. They're speaking a dialect I can't understand."

The Métis ignored Peggy. They stopped talking and stared through the open door into the land office. Then, at an order of the oldest of the group, they slowly retreated out to the street and climbed up onto their horses, which were tethered at a rail in front of the building. As the Bains family watched the group ride away, each one felt a sense of unease. Manitoba was said to be a place of opportunity and freedom. Now it seemed hopelessly divided and dangerous.

"Anyone else wanting to register land?" the clerk called out from his office.

Cautiously, Peggy Bains ventured in through the door, followed by her four children.

The clerk, perched on a high stool behind a roll-top desk, now wore a green visor on his forehead. He was still irritated. "Those Métis are born troublemakers," he said more to himself than anyone who might be listening.

"But why did you treat them like that?" Peggy asked, still shocked at the exchange.

"They will kill us in our sleep if we're not careful," he replied before turning to the business at hand. "Yes, madam. How may I help you?"

It took Peggy a moment to gather her thoughts. She could argue with the clerk about his treatment of the Métis, but more than anything else they needed land. "I've come to take out a homestead in the Portage la Prairie district," she said with all the confidence she could muster. "We intend to build a family farm."

"Where is the head of the family?"

"I am Peggy Bains, a widow. These are my children." She knew that she had to speak with authority if she was to gain respect in this frontier dominated by men.

The clerk's eyebrows arched upwards and he said, "Women don't have the strength or stamina for homesteading."

Peggy stayed perfectly calm. "But the Act says that any person who is the head of a family and over twenty-one is entitled to a quarter section of land."

"It shouldn't be allowed. Even strong young men have a hard time homesteading on the prairie."

Meg was not about to accept this. "We're eligible according to the law," she interrupted. "My mother is the head of our family."

"Meg …" Peggy tried to shush her oldest daughter, but it did no good.

"Are you saying my mother's not a person?" she continued. Meg's habit of standing up for her rights often got her into trouble.

"Well, no. It's just that homesteading is brutal work. Only the strongest survive."

"That's up to us. We want our land."

The clerk hesitated for a moment. "Well, if you insist. I can't stop you. But don't let anyone say I didn't warn you."

Peggy smiled with relief. This was the first bit of good news they had heard since they got to Winnipeg.

"Snap to it," the clerk said impatiently. "Pick your quarter section. I don't have all day."

A map of the Portage district was produced that showed the land marked off in neat squares with perfectly straight lines. Each square was a quarter section of land of 160 acres. They had to pick one that no one else had claimed. Finally, after much family discussion, they made their choice of a quarter section south of the Assiniboine River. Peggy paid the ten-dollar registration fee, then they were given a map and issued a piece of paper for the land that they had selected.

When they got back out onto the muddy street, Peggy could barely contain her excitement. "Land … we finally have land of our very own!"

Financial security had been Peggy's dream for a long time. After her husband's death in a logging camp, she had taken in laundry to support the family and had seen her children, John, Meg, and Jamie, scatter across the country in an effort to find work. They had laboured in factories and logging camps, and on ships, fishing boats, and railways, but all they gained was a poverty-level survival. John, the oldest, was still away in Newfoundland, and the other members of the family did not know if they would ever see him again.

"But where is this land?" asked Kate cautiously.

"Three days travel to the west."

"Three more days ...?" It seemed they had been travelling for months and still they were no closer to the farm.

For Peggy, that piece of paper granting them land was the conclusion of months of planning, scrimping, and saving. She had hoarded her pennies, patched their clothes, saved and cut corners in every possible way until she finally had enough money for this venture. Two weeks before, Kate, Robbie, and Peggy had left their home in Ottawa by train and travelled to London, in southwestern Ontario, where they met Meg and Jamie. Then the five of them left to start their new life in the Canadian west.

The family came out on the train via Chicago and arrived in St. Paul, Minnesota, in April, exhausted from the trip. There Robbie, the youngest of the family at age ten, got sick with fever. They had to stay in a small room over a saloon for five days until Peggy and Meg nursed him back to health. They would have dug into their precious resources if Jamie and Kate had not gone out to sell newspapers on the street corners to earn enough for them to survive.

When Robbie was well enough to travel, the family took the train up to Fisher's Landing on the Red River and came down river to Winnipeg aboard the paddle steamer *Selkirk*. When the Bains family arrived it was early May, not a day to lose if they were to get their land and plant a crop for the season.

"I want to be on the road by tonight," their mother announced to the children. "We have to get organized. The first thing to do is buy an ox and a Red River cart."

"But horses are the only thing, Mother," said Jamie impatiently. "They're fast and strong. You can hitch them to a wagon or saddle them for riding. Oxen are so slow, we may never get to our farm." Jamie had worked in a livery stable and felt that horses were the answer to all of their needs.

"No," said his mother. "I grew up on a farm, Jamie, and I know something about what we will need."

The boy was sure that his mother was wrong, but he knew that there was no arguing with her now.

The family walked down to the market and met a Métis with an ox and cart for sale. Once the man found the family could speak French, he became friendly. After a long inspection and haggling, he agreed to a price of fifty dollars and threw in a walking plough to sweeten the deal. The arrangement pleased Peggy.

Next was a trip to the general store to buy supplies such as flour, oats for porridge, salt pork, milk, and other provisions. Seed for the garden was also purchased: potatoes, turnip, squash, peas, beans, corn, carrots, and pumpkins. It was a long list. Finally they visited a hardware store, where they bought some badly needed tools.

Once they had everything loaded into the Red River cart, they were ready to set off. But before they left Winnipeg, Peggy mailed a quick note to John listing the lot they had been issued. It was mid-afternoon when the Bains family headed out of the town toward Portage la Prairie.

The road went west, following the north bank of the Assiniboine River, through oak groves and past farms of the Selkirk settlers. It was used by Métis driving heavily loaded carts to Fort Edmonton and was badly rutted. The ungreased axle of the Red River cart screeched with every turn. The ox lumbered on so slowly that the young members of the Bains family often got bored and tired of the effort.

Often Jamie, Kate, and Robbie walked a long way ahead to explore the trail and then sit in a grove of trees to wait for the others to catch up. At night all five of them slept under the cart with their feet to the fire, trying to keep warm while the ox quietly grazed nearby.

On the second day, to break the boredom, Peggy Bains suggested that they choose a name for the big ox. Jamie suggested "Slowpoke" or "Full Stop." Then, in a twist of sarcasm, suggested "Speedy," but no one liked any of these names. Finally they agreed on "Baby," a suggestion made by Robbie, who explained that the big ox was the newest and most gentle member of the family.

Jamie only started to warm up to Baby after they went across the ford of the Assiniboine River, west of the town of Portage la Prairie. The current was strong with the spring run-off. The whole family climbed on board the cart to stay dry, and Baby plodded into the water. The strong current pulled at the ox and threatened to sweep the cart away, but Baby kept moving through the water without pause.

"We're going to lose the load!" Jamie shouted. He was about to slip over the side into the cold water and swim for shore when his mother's hand grabbed him firmly and held him in place.

The water rose up over the stomach of the ox, and for a moment it seemed as if it would surge into the cart.

"We could be swept away!" Jamie yelled again.

For a second the whole cart began to float, and it looked like it could be swept down river with the current, but the big ox kept plodding along until the big wheels of the cart hit bottom again and rose up on the other bank. They were on solid ground again.

Jamie was impressed. "I thought we would lose everything."

His mother felt vindicated. "You've got to have a little faith, Jamie. Not only is an ox strong, but it is the most reliable animal you can own."

The trail leading away from the ford was a steep incline. Baby strained to pull the Red River cart up the hill.

"Come on!" Peggy Bains shouted to her children. "We have to work together to get to the top."

The family scrambled down from the top of the cart. Jamie pushed on one of the creaking wooden wheels while Meg strained against the other. Peggy put her back to the cart, pushing with all of her strength. Kate and Robbie strained on either side of her. The powerful ox leaned his body into the yoke, and slowly the cart moved up the rough trail. They plodded, one step at a time, until finally they reached the top and could stop and rest.

The open prairie spread out before them. The grassland stretched as far as the eye could see, waving in the gentle breeze until it met and merged with the blue sky at the horizon. Behind them, along the river and up the bank, was a forest of poplar, aspen, oak, and dogwood. Scattered on the prairie were clumps of trees giving a parkland look to the scene. Overhead an eagle circled in the bright cloudless sky as it patiently searched for prey.

"It sure looks empty," said Jamie, more to himself than the others.

"It's beautiful," replied his mother, Peggy. "This is the place where our family can start to build a new life."

"Are we sure we want to live here?" asked Robbie sceptically. To the young boy, the prairie seemed devoid of life.

"What's wrong?" Meg asked her younger brother.

"There's no neighbours. There won't be anyone my age."

Peggy smiled at her brood and said, "Someday there will be other families and schools — lots of houses and roads to travel on. But first we have to establish our farm and support ourselves." Their mother's incurable optimism gave the others a lift. "Let's stop sightseeing. We've got a lot to do before this day is out."

"How are we ever going to find our farm?" Jamie asked, staring across the empty prairie.

Meg got out the map they had been given at the land office and spread it out on the ground while the rest of the family gathered around.

"Here's the ford of the river, and the trail going up the hill." She traced the route on the map with her finger. "There's our farm away over here."

They counted eight quarter sections south and three quarter sections to the east between the spot they were standing and their farm. Meg stood up, looked around for a moment and then pointed toward the southeast. "Our homestead has to be in that direction," she concluded.

The others looked at the map and then at the landscape and back at the map again. They discussed the situation thoroughly before finally agreeing that Meg was right. Peggy's excitement brought it to an end. "Let's go and find our new home!"

Meg prodded Baby with a stick, and the cart left the trail, heading southeast across the virgin prairie. The ox plodded along at his usual leisurely pace. The axle squealed as the large wheels of the Red River cart rolled over the fresh spring grass, marking a new trail as they went.

It was mid-afternoon and the May sun, shining out of a cloudless sky, made the Bains family hot. From the west a gentle breeze brought a cool, refreshing smell on the air. Flowers were everywhere: blue, yellow, pink, and white. Kate began gathering them and soon had a huge armful that she presented to her mother. Peggy smiled at the generous gesture of her youngest daughter.

Kate was thirteen years old, that awkward age where she was still unsure of herself. She had a quick smile and long auburn hair like her mother. All the way out to Manitoba, she had complained about the move, but now, seeing the open prairie and the vast western sky, she felt a rising excitement.

At first the prairie had seemed empty, but as they moved across it they found the place alive with wildlife. A prairie chicken startled them as it flew up out of the heavy grass, but it disappeared as quickly as it had come. Overhead, geese and ducks were flying north on their long migration back to their nesting grounds. The long grass was filled with crickets and grasshoppers, snakes and gophers.

The three youngest children fanned out in front of the cart as they attempted to find the surveyor's stakes marking the boundary lines of the quarter sections. Peggy was worried that Robbie might get lost in the long grass and made him ride on top of the cart. He was a delicate, dreamy, ten-year-old boy, who seemed more at home in his books than out on the raw prairie.

Jamie and Kate roamed a long way ahead of the others. Kate discovered an iron stake in the ground with writing on the side and called to the others. Meg studied the marking and then looked at the map for the longest time to pinpoint their location. "It's another mile and a half due south to our homestead," she announced.

Peggy could barely contain her excitement. After all the months and years of work and planning, scrimping and saving, they were finally going to find their own land. "It's our land, Meg. Ours! Think of it!" she said, unable to contain her excitement.

Kate was having a difficult time on the rough ground. Her long skirt got caught in the grass and almost tripped her a number of times. Once she kicked at a white object in the grass and found the bleached skull and horns of a buffalo.

They were a long way ahead of the others when they heard their mother shouting to them. "What did she say?" Jamie asked.

"I think she said don't get lost, or stay together. Something like that."

Kate liked being with her older brother. When they had been little, living in Ottawa, they had been very close. But Jamie had worked away from home for more than a year. He was fourteen years old. In the last year, he had grown four inches and was almost as tall as their mother. Kate found her brother quieter than she remembered. He was attentive to detail, with restless blue eyes constantly watching and trying to understand. She wondered if she would ever be like that.

"Look," Jamie called to his sister. He had found another iron stake in the ground. He stood up, glancing back to where they had come from and then gazing ahead. "One more mile due south, and we'll be on our land!" He felt a rush of excitement.

"Come on, I'll race you to it!" Kate shouted with a laugh. She hitched up her long skirt and began to run through the long grass, an infectious giggle flowing behind her. "I'll be the first to the homestead!"

"Come back, Kate! You might get lost!" But Jamie was laughing, too. He followed her at a run and soon caught up to his sister. "Why are you so slow?"

She had her skirt pulled up well over her knees. She wasn't going to let this brother of hers win the race. Kate sprinted as fast and as hard as she could until she caught him. Now the two of them ran together, happy to be free and alive on this untouched prairie.

The land rose a little and then fell away. As they came to the top of the rise, they could see a vast parklike stretch of prairie. In front of them, not ten paces away, was the iron stake marking the beginning of their property. The two of them saw the stake at the same time. With a cry they sprinted toward it until they both fell at the marker, laughing and rolling in the long grass.

"I got here first!" shouted Kate.

"Did not. Beat you by a mile!"

They laughed for a minute as they rolled on the soft grass. Then, gradually they stopped and slowly, without a word, got to their feet. This was going to be their home. What did it look like?

The green prairie rolled on endlessly. In the east of the property, a clump of trees grew along a creek. Not far away, ten or more horses stood grazing quietly, watching them with curiosity.

"Where did those horses come from?" Kate asked. "Are they wild?"

Jamie stared at them with the studied eye of the horseman. These were more like ponies than horses. They were much smaller than the draft horses used in farming and even smaller than the riding horses that he had worked with in Ontario, but they were strong animals with big chests and lean haunches. They looked as if they could run for hours and survive the worst winter on the prairie.

Jamie took a few steps toward the animals. It was only as they shied away that he noticed that their legs were hobbled so they could be easily caught. These were not wild horses. Someone was grazing them on their land.

"What is it, Jamie?" Kate asked as she came up beside him.

The boy was about to explain when he spotted a horseman in the distance riding straight toward them at a hard gallop. Jamie wondered for a moment if they had been stalked and hunted. As the horseman came closer, they could see that he was young, no more than twenty years old. He had a dark complexion, more Indian than white, and he wore a tan pull-over shirt with a colourful red sash tied around his waist, signalling that he was a Métis. A big sunhat, pulled over his forehead, did not hide the fury and determination in his face.

Kate grasped her brother's arm in panic. The horse thundered down on them. At the last moment, the man turned his mount and brought it to a stop in a cloud of dust.

"What you doing here?" the man demanded in halting English. His horse trembled and was soaked in a lather.

Jamie tried to stay calm. "Are those your horses?" he asked.

"Métis have pasture rights on these lands!" The young man shouted in anger as his horse danced about nervously.

"This is our homestead," said Kate impulsively. "That's our marker right there." She pointed at the iron stake. "Mother has all the papers to prove it."

The man's horse kicked violently and reared back on its hind legs, but the horseman never lost control. "It has always been our land to graze our horses and cattle," he announced with a loud voice. "Even with your piece of paper, you have no rights here. This will always be the land of the Métis people!"

Just at that moment the Red River cart, with the other members of the family, crested the rise.

# 2

Robbie sat high up on the Red River cart, and Meg and Peggy walked on either side of the big ox as they lumbered slowly up to the others and came to a halt.

The horseman swept off his big hat, and his long dark hair flowed out almost to his shoulders. Years of riding on the prairie had given his young face a handsome, weather-beaten look. His anger made him look proud and defiant. "Who is the leader of this group?" he demanded in his heavy French accent.

"What's the problem?" Peggy asked calmly.

The rider's horse danced about impatiently. Kate and Jamie joined their mother to avoid the horse and its sharp hooves. "This is our land," the young man repeated. "The Dauphin family has hay privileges. Métis have the right to graze their horses over all of this land." He swept his hat indicating the vast prairie.

"We've been granted the right to homestead here," Meg said, walking toward the horseman. "That iron stake marks the beginning of our land."

"Métis have always had grazing rights! We need the land for our buffalo ponies."

"Show him the paper, Mother." Meg was standing in front of him, her hands on her hips.

"Papers, they are nothing! You English cut up the land into neat squares for your farms, and tear up the natural order of things! Métis will not put up with it!"

"This is our land now!" Meg said, equally defiant.

The Métis horse shied away, and the rider fought to bring it under control. "We'll see!" he shouted.

He swept his hat back onto his head and gave a quick kick to the animal's ribs. The high-spirited horse reared back for a moment, as if to throw the rider off, then he leapt into a gallop, his hooves pounding on the hard prairie. The horse and rider raced as hard as they could back toward the trees that marked the Assiniboine River. The Bains family watched him go without uttering a word.

"Why did he say all those things?" asked Kate, finally. "Is it really not our land?"

"Of course it's our land," replied Meg. "It was given to us by the government."

Peggy watched the horseman until he had almost disappeared. What did all this mean? First there were the men in the land office and now this. The Métis claimed the prairie as grazing land, but the family was committed to its plan of homesteading. She was worried, but there was no turning back now.

"Let's get organized," she said brightly, trying to change the sombre mood of the family. "We've got a lot of work to do before sundown. Jamie, have you found a good place to set up camp?"

"It looks like there's a stream over by those trees."

"Good. Let's set up camp over there."

They got the cart rolling again, and in a few minutes came to the clump of trees. Jamie and Kate had scouted ahead and found a small stream no more than a yard wide with a slow-moving current. The water was clean and clear.

Jamie picked a spot to camp upstream from where the horses came down to drink. A broad grassy spot under an old oak tree provided shade and shelter from the wind. Meg guided the ox in under the tree. They unshackled the cart and took off the yoke to let Baby wander freely. With the hard work of the day, his rest was well deserved.

Everyone had chores. Jamie got out the shovel and began to dig a fire pit. Peggy and Meg took down the wooden boxes and sacks containing their food. Nothing was more precious than this. With their money almost exhausted, they would need to harbour every bit of food that they owned. Kate and Robbie got the sheet of canvas and spread it on the ground. By that time Jamie had finished digging the pit and came to help them.

They scouted around, looking for poles to hang up the canvas, but on that almost treeless plain they were nonexistent. Finally, at their mother's suggestion, they tied one corner of the canvas to the tree, another to the cart, and staked the other two corners to the ground to make a lean-to. The shelter was big enough for them to sleep in and during the day there was room to store things under the canvas. It would have to do until they built something more permanent.

The sun was beginning to sink, and everyone was hungry. They had last eaten when they were on the trail, hours before. The three youngest were sent off to find firewood, but without much success. There were a few twigs under the trees along the creek. Robbie found one fair-sized dead branch, but there was not enough wood to make a half-decent cooking fire.

The three of them began to scout out on the prairie. Kate was the first to come across bones — the remains of the vast buffalo herds that had grazed on the prairie grass for thousands of years. They began gathering the bones to burn in the fire. Then Jamie started finding buffalo chips — lots of them.

"What is it?" Robbie asked.

"Dried buffalo dung," Jamie explained, and when Robbie and Kate curled their noses in disgust, he added, "This stuff will burn best of all."

He was right. Once they got the buffalo chips going with burning twigs and grass, they gave out a hot blue flame that was perfect for cooking. The two young ones were still disgusted, but they relented when Jamie told them that this would save them an enormous amount of work.

Soon their mother had bannock cooking over the fire. It was plain fare: flour and water cooked in a pan with a tight-fitting lid. There was no yeast in the mixture, so it did not rise like bread, but for those who were hungry, bannock smeared with a little lard and sprinkled with salt tasted delicious. Peggy served it with thin slices of salt pork and a cup of black unsweetened tea.

The Bains family sat around the fire pit chatting as they ate. A few clouds had gathered in the western sky, and as the sun slowly sank, the fringes of the clouds took on spectacular colours of red, gold, and orange. Gradually the light faded, the breeze dropped, and the land darkened.

Peggy spoke softly into the gathering evening, "Arriving here, on our own land, is the end of a long journey, but also the start of a new life for us." She was thoughtful for a few moments.

She was only in her mid-thirties, but already there had been much hardship in her life. Peggy knew that this Manitoba homestead was their one chance to build a secure future. Still, she was worried. Favourable weather and good luck were as important as planning and hard work to make a success of farming. Would the elements be in their favour or not?

She got to her feet, undid her auburn hair and let it fall down her back. As she stretched her tall lean body, she smiled at her four children gathered around the fire. "Let's get some sleep. We've got a lot of work ahead of us."

That first night under the canvas lean-to was cold. The temperature dropped close to freezing, and the fire did not provide much warmth. The family members snuggled together under their blankets. Jamie, who was on the outside, was shivering by daybreak. He got up to stir the fire and put on some extra clothes. He walked around until the sun came over the horizon and finally warmed his bones.

By the time the others were up, the boy had a pot of water heating over the fire. Their mother made a big pot of oatmeal porridge, which they ate with a little lard. They had run out of milk two days before.

"Sure would be nice to have some sugar," Meg commented.

"We've got to get some income off this land before we can afford luxuries like that," Peggy replied with a laugh, but the comment reminded her of her worries. Would they have enough money to survive until the harvest?

She insisted that the camp be clean and tidy. Everyone, even the youngest, had chores to complete. Then Peggy announced her plan for the day.

"This morning we're going to look at our property. We have to decide where to build our house and barn and where we're going to plant our crops."

All morning they walked along the property lines inspecting the fields and creek bed. The land was flat, especially the southern half of it, but it was well drained.

Peggy felt that one of the biggest assets was the creek. "Even if it dries up in summer, it means the water table is not far below. We should be able to dig a well without any problem."

"But where are we going to put the house?" asked Kate.

"Right in the middle of the farm," said Robbie. That way we won't have far to walk to any part of the property."

"Well, I think we should be down by the stream. Then we won't have far to walk for water."

"I don't know, Jamie," said their mother thoughtfully. "If there is a heavy snowfall, the stream could rise and there could be flooding."

The others deferred to her experience, and they picked a spot a fair distance back from the stream.

Next they had to decide where to plough the fields for their crops. "This is even more important than the house," Peggy argued. "We have less than four weeks to get our crops seeded or they will never ripen before the fall."

Kate was alarmed. "We'll never be able to plant all 160 acres of the farm."

Her mother laughed. "We'll be lucky to plant a five-acre field. Let's find the best land possible. Jamie, get the shovel."

The family walked all around the homestead again. In several spots Jamie dug holes in the ground. In every hole Peggy would reach down, bring up earth, and let it run between her fingers. At each hole she repeated the same thing, "Loam — good black loam. The best growing earth in the world." The more holes they dug, the more excited she became.

Meg voiced one worry. "The real question is will it grow anything or is it too dry and cold out here on the prairies?"

"If Red Fife wheat can grow in the Ottawa Valley, it can grow on the prairies. I'm sure of it."

But Peggy was not as certain as she pretended. She had read everything she could find about farming in Manitoba and decided that hard spring wheat would be the best for the climate. Before she left home, she had gone to a seed mill and bought a bag of Red Fife seed. All the way out on the trip she had guarded this seed and talked about it endlessly with her children. The family's future depended on it, she would tell them, but she never admitted to anyone that there was a possibility that the crop could be a total failure.

Meg did not know what to think about wheat, but she was interested in a vegetable garden. Potatoes, carrots, turnips, corn, squash — these were things that she felt were worth growing because they would feed the family through the winter. They had bought enough seeds for a big garden when they were in Winnipeg. Meg was anxious to get them in the ground.

Over a lunch of cold bannock, they decided they would put the vegetable garden close to the house, where they could watch it in case birds or animals decided to make a meal of it before they did.

After lunch Peggy got the walking plough out of the cart with Jamie's help, and the two began an inspection. It was well used and banged up. The metal blade that cut the sod was dull and nicks had been taken out of it. Jamie got the metal file they had bought and began the slow process of sharpening the blade.

Kate and Robbie found themselves with nothing to do for a moment and escaped before their mother assigned them a job. Robbie was interested in the beautiful yellow meadowlarks that darted everywhere. They had wandered quite a distance from the camp when they spotted a horseman riding toward them from the west.

At first they thought it could be the Métis man coming back. They hid in the long grass to spy on him, but as he got closer they realized that the man was riding a big black workhorse that lumbered along slowly, not the fast buffalo pony of the Métis. The two ran back to camp announcing that a man was approaching.

As he came closer, it was obvious that this was a farmer. He wore heavy work pants held up with suspenders, a blue shirt, and a broad-brimmed felt hat. A shaggy mustache and long sideburns covered much of his face. The farmer's horse was a huge cumbersome draft horse that was slow but looked immensely strong.

"Campbell's my name," he said as he slid off the back of his horse. "Wilf Campbell. Our homestead's about four miles to the west of you here. I saw smoke coming up from here last night, and I thought I would come and investigate." He had a pleasant smile and a friendly manner.

"We're neighbours then," Peggy replied as she shook his hand. "We've taken this quarter section of land. Just arrived yesterday."

"I'll be ..." Campbell said laughing. "The prairies are fillin' up all of a sudden. Couple of bachelors took home-steads near us. Just arrived days ago. Soon we'll have a city bustin' at the seams." He spoke with a relaxed drawl that put the others at ease.

Peggy introduced all the members of the family from Meg, the oldest, to Robbie, the youngest.

"Well, now, sure is a pleasure. Got children myself, four young ones always underfoot with a good wife to run after them and all. But where's the man of the family?"

"I'm ... I'm a widow," Peggy replied hesitantly.

"A widow woman out here homesteadin' on the prairie by herself?" he said, with a sceptical note in his voice. "Field work is mighty hard. You'll need a man to do the heavy labour."

"We can do it," Peggy countered, but she did not sound very convincing.

"Never heard it done before."

"We will do it, Mr. Campbell," said Meg with that deter-mined look on her face that the family had learned to respect.

"She's a mighty tough go out here, especially at plantin' time and harvest and in the middle of the winter. Why, it gets so cold here that hot tea will freeze in the cup before you can get it to your lips. It's full-time work just to stay alive. I know. This is my third season in Manitoba."

"Would you like some tea, Mr. Campbell? It won't freeze on a day like today." Peggy was anxious to change the subject before their neighbour painted a picture of complete gloom.

"Don't mind if I do. It's always a thirsty ride across the prairie."

The youngest stirred up the fire, filled the pot with water out of the creek, and set it to boil. The others sat in the background listening while Meg and the adults talked.

Mr. Campbell related how he had brought his family out from Ontario to get free land. They had managed to get a house and barn built, and he planned to range cattle and dairy cows.

"We're going to put in Red Fife wheat," said Peggy confidently.

"I don't know about wheat," Campbell said with a doubting tone. "Growin' season's awful short in these parts. Even vegetables have a hard time of it."

"But this is all grasslands and wheat is a type of grass."

"Frost can come in mid-September 'round here. Could wipe you out before the grain is even ripe."

"Red Fife, Mr. Campbell. That's the answer."

They sipped on their tea and chatted pleasantly about things back in Ontario and life out on the prairies. Then Meg changed the subject.

"Yesterday, when we arrived, there was a Métis man here. He said that he had pasture rights on our land."

"Was he young?"

"Around twenty years old. He was riding a bay-coloured horse."

"Dauphin. That's the family. Louis Dauphin. I saw their ponies when I rode in. Real trouble that family. All the Métis hereabouts are trouble. They had Manitoba all in a stir about six or seven years ago. Louis Riel — what a problem. Tried to stop the survey of the land. Opposed to us homesteaders. They're just troublemakers. That's all."

"We met some other Métis," Meg added. "They seem to think that English settlers are taking their land."

"They're French and Catholic and opposed to us English and Protestant. That's what it is."

"But if their land is being taken from them …"

"They never farmed this land!" Campbell was getting agitated. "Their farms are just along the river. They used this land to graze their ponies. They didn't own it, and they never had title to it. Now that the buffalo are gone they won't need this land anymore."

He looked angry just talking about the issue. "Let me warn you. Them Métis are treacherous. They killed young Thomas Scott, and they'll kill us all if we're not careful."

Campbell stood up and finished his black tea in one gulp. He smiled. "Nice to have more neighbours, I must say. Friends for the young ones."

"Are there any plans for a school?" asked Peggy.

"Have to ask the wife about that. I look after the farm. She looks after the children. That's the way we work," he said, mounting his big draft horse.

"We look after everything together, Mr. Campbell," said Peggy, smiling. "That's the way we work."

"Everyone's different, I guess. Anyway, nice to meet you. Sure hope you can make a go of this place." With a wave, his big lumbering beast broke into a slow trot, and the farmer headed back to his homestead in the west.

# 3

---

Jamie continued the tedious task of sharpening the cutting blade on the plough while the others went off to begin the building of their sod house.

Peggy stood at the spot they had selected and explained. "The house has to be dug three feet into the earth. Then the walls are built up with sod clumps that we dig out of the ground."

"Are we really going to live in a hole in the ground, Mummy?" asked Robbie unhappily.

She tried to be cheerful. "It will be really nice and cosy and warm — especially in winter when it gets so cold here."

"We'll be living like those gopher things that we see popping their heads up out of the ground."

"It won't be so bad. Come on. Let's mark out the house."

Peggy had brought some string, and they carefully outlined the walls of the house by stretching string along the ground and pegging it into place. When they finished, they stood back to get a view. The prospective house looked small, about twenty feet by fifteen feet.

"It will be a lot of digging," said Meg.

"I know," replied her mother, "but there is no other way."

Peggy took the shovel and stepped inside the rectangle marked out with the string. She positioned the shovel and made the first cut into the sod. Carefully she cut out a square and then levered it up with the shovel. Meg reached in with her hands to tear it away from its roots. It took real effort of pulling and cutting at the roots with the shovel before the square of sod came free. Then they piled it on the string where the wall was to be built.

Slowly Meg and Peggy began working, one square of sod at a time, along in a row. By the time they had cut away five sod squares, they were both dirty and covered in sweat. When it was time to quit for supper, only one row of sod, the length of the house, had been cut and stacked.

"It's going to take forever," said Kate, who had been watching closely.

"We've got to keep going," replied Meg, adopting the role of mother.

Jamie worked on the walking plough until nightfall before finally announcing that he had done all he could to sharpen the steel. "It looks like new," his mother said, putting her arm around his shoulders. "I just hope it works. We don't have time to fix equipment. We've got to get that crop into the ground."

That night it was a little warmer. There were a few black flies that bothered them, but they were all so tired that they slept soundly. Peggy was up before the dawn. She let her children sleep for a while. They were going to need all the rest they could get.

In the dim light of the cool dawn, she rummaged around in her travelling box and pulled out the work clothes that she had brought along for ploughing. First she put on a heavy denim shirt and then pulled on a baggy pair of men's long, heavy trousers. She fastened them over her shoulders with suspenders. Finally she combed her long hair, wrapped it around her head in a tight bun, and placed a floppy sunhat on her head.

Peggy felt strange in this outfit. She had never worn anything in her life except long skirts. Now she looked like a farmer dressed for working in the fields. But it was necessary, she told herself. Essential.

"Jamie … Jamie …" she called, shaking her son awake.

The dawn was just breaking on another beautiful prairie morning. In the east the sky was a brilliant orange. Gradually the land lost its darkness and became sharper and brighter.

"What is it?" the boy asked, fighting against sleep.

"I need you to help me hitch up the ox."

"Why are you dressed like that?"

"We start ploughing today."

Jamie dressed and went off to find Baby. A few minutes later, he returned with the big lumbering beast. They fixed the yoke over his head and attached the plough through a rig of chains and shackles.

Peggy had put on water to make porridge, and by the time the ox was rigged up, it was ready. Meg scrambled out of bed to join them. Kate was awake, but she snuggled into the blanket beside her sleeping brother to stay warm.

"Do you think you can do the ploughing all by yourself?" Meg asked her mother.

"Who else? We don't have any money for a hired hand."

After eating, they set off with Baby dragging the plough to the spot where they had planned their first field. The two youngest members of the family got up and dressed before they left camp. They ate breakfast in a rush and then ran to join the others just as they were getting ready to begin the first furrow. They thought that their mother's outfit looked funny, but she was far too serious for them to dare say anything.

Peggy was concerned about steering the ox once ploughing started. When they were on the trail, they could walk beside Baby, and he would follow, but when they were ploughing the driver was behind the ox, handling the plough. How could they direct him from back there? They positioned Baby so that he was heading straight down the field and pulled and tugged on the plough until it was in the right position. They were ready to start.

Peggy leaned her weight on the handles of the plough. "Gee up," she called. "Come on, Baby, move!" But the big animal did nothing. "Jamie, you've got to steer him until the first furrow is ploughed."

The boy had brought a stick just for this purpose. He prodded Baby just once, and the big ox began to walk steadily. The chains and shackles rattled as they grew taut. Peggy leaned on the handles, the plough pulled down into the soil and began to cut through the sod. The earth curled over, and a black furrow was cut into the grassland.

It was all Peggy could do to hold the handles of the plough upright. She could feel the strength of the ox as he pulled it through the ground. The handles lurched and twisted from the force of the pull, and she struggled to hold them straight as best she could. Peggy walked behind the plough at the pace of Baby, pulling on the handles one way and then the other in a determined effort to keep the plough upright and keep the furrow straight. The entire Bains family walked with her while the scar of the furrow was cut across the prairie. Finally, after two hundred yards or more, Peggy signalled to stop. Jamie stepped in front of the ox, and the ploughing came to an immediate halt.

Peggy's shoulders ached as she turned back to look at the first furrow she had cut into their land. It was a little crooked in places, but that did not really matter. The earth was a consistent black loam.

She smiled broadly at her brood gathered around her. "It's good," she said. "Better than I even hoped for. Baby and the plough worked wonderfully."

They repositioned the plough beside the first furrow and headed back in the direction they had come. Slowly the plough turned over another neat furrow. When they finished,

Peggy's muscles ached from the effort of holding the plough, but she was enthusiastic. "Baby must have pulled a plough before," she remarked. "He seems to know what to do. I think I can handle him without any trouble. Why don't the rest of you go back and continue the digging for the house?"

The others were not exactly pleased. Digging the hole was hard work. There was a chorus of complaints from Jamie and Kate. "Come on," said Meg. "The house won't get finished by itself."

By midday they had stripped the tough prairie grass from about half of the area of the house. Jamie did most of the digging, with Meg pulling and tearing at the pieces of sod and then stacking them neatly to make the walls.

As she worked, Meg was quiet and brooding. She was only sixteen, but she had lived independently for a long time and now that she was back with the family she had to play the role of older sister. She was not sure she was happy with that. Would she always live on the farm, isolated from the cities and other people her age? Did she want to live this type of life? She was confused and uncertain.

As she worked, she pushed her long blond hair out of her eyes. She was a young woman now. She had changed from a girl, when she had first left the family two years before, into a tall woman with striking blond hair, healthy bronzed skin, and a strength in both body and spirit.

When the sun was high in the sky, the four of them stopped work and walked over to the field. Their mother was just finishing the sixth furrow. She was exhausted and slumped into the grass. "Wrestling with the plough is sure hard work."

"You've been at it for six hours or more," Meg replied. "It's no wonder that you're tired."

They unshackled Baby to let him graze. The children sat in the grass beside their mother and stared up at the billowy clouds that drifted across the blue sky. A minute later Kate noticed that their mother had fallen fast asleep. Peggy looked strangely innocent in her men's work clothes, with her hair bound up on top of her head. Sleep drained away the worry and exhaustion from her face.

"She's totally done in," said Meg. "Robbie, you stay with her. The rest of us will go and make some lunch."

They got bannock and salt pork, and a big jug of cold water from the creek, and carried them down to the spot where their mother lay sleeping. She woke, and they had a picnic in the grass. It was warm and pleasant in that place. The crickets hummed, and the long grass was alive with birds and small creatures.

As soon as the lunch was over, Peggy got to her feet. "I have to keep ploughing."

"Rest a little longer," urged Meg.

"The more we seed, the bigger our crop in the fall." With Jamie's help, she hitched the plough to the ox and began another furrow.

After lunch Meg and Jamie returned to the back-breaking chore of digging the hole for the sod house. Robbie and Kate carried the picnic things back to camp and then sat around. There was not much for them to do, and they soon got bored. Robbie read one of the precious books he had brought, and his sister wandered onto the prairie to explore.

The long grass hid a broad variety of life. Kate spotted a rabbit and chased it until it disappeared into a hole in the ground. A prairie chicken came running along, spotted her, turned and ran as fast as it could in the opposite direction.

The gophers were fascinating. Kate spotted one looking at her as it perched on the edge of its burrow. It disappeared down its hole as soon as she moved. Carefully she crept up close and lay on the ground right at the entrance to its burrow. Sure enough, the gopher was so curious it popped its head out only to see Kate's face inches away. She laughed, but the gopher poked its head out several times before the girl got bored and moved on.

Kate plucked a white daisy and picked off the petals as she wandered along thinking about what life was going to be like on the homestead. She felt a sense of freedom in this place. How she hated the long dress she had to wear that caught at her ankles as she walked through the long prairie grass. Impulsively Kate undid her hair and let it flow in a long auburn cascade down to the small of her back.

She was so self-absorbed that she was surprised when she found herself only yards away from the Métis ponies. They stirred as they watched her approach.

Kate counted ten horses altogether. There were mares and stallions. They were thinner than most horses because they had been left to range on the prairie all winter long. It would take the summer of grazing to get them in good condition again but most looked young and fast.

One of the horses was a young stallion, a little bigger than the others. He was a tan colour with big dark spots on his back and sides. His mane and tail were nearly black. Kate moved closer, trying not to spook the pony. He stood stock-still, his head erect, ears alert, watching every motion that she made. She moved as quietly as she could until she was standing right beside the tan and black pony. Kate stood a few inches taller than the pony and as she moved her hand up to pat his neck, he suddenly danced away. She was so startled she jumped.

The horse and girl eyed each other for a minute or more before Kate slowly began approaching him again. She was not sure why she felt drawn to this wild, sensitive animal. She just felt the need to reach out to him. This time she approached with all the patience in the world. Slowly she moved beside him and gently began stroking his neck while talking soothingly.

"There … there. That's a good pony. There's nothing to be frightened about. I just want to stroke your long beautiful neck." As she talked, she noticed that the mane and tail of the horse were matted and filled with burrs.

Jamie was still digging the hole for the house when he began to wonder where his sister had disappeared to. Kate had been gone for some time, and this was a wild and strange country. "Maybe I'd better go and look for her," he said to Meg.

"Kate's an independent type. She'll be all right."

"But she could get lost. There are no landmarks out there."

"Well, don't take all day, Jamie. I need your help."

The boy was glad to escape. They still had not stripped all the sod for the house, and he was tired of the heavy work. He brushed himself off as best he could and hiked out in the direction Kate had disappeared.

Jamie found her standing beside the tan and black pony, gently stroking his neck and back. The pony heard his approach, pricked up his ears, and looked around. Kate waved at him, trying to signal that he should approach cautiously.

"Why have you been away so long?" Jamie asked sharply.

The horse bolted away limping from the hobble on his front legs. He stopped a few yards away and watched them.

"Now look what you've done." Kate was cross.

"He's just a horse."

"Look at his markings, Jamie. He's beautiful."

The boy looked closely at the horse for the first time. "He sure is different all right."

"I think he's the most beautiful horse that I've ever seen." Kate had moved beside the pony again and was stroking his neck. "Do you think we could ride him, Jamie?"

"He belongs to the Métis, and you heard what Mr. Campbell said about them."

"Just one little ride. No one will ever know."

"But what if something happened?"

"Like what? You're a horseman, Jamie. You said that you can ride any type of horse."

"Well yeah, but …" Jamie moved slowly toward his sister and the nervous pony. He did know a lot about horses, but this one was very shy and skittish. He wondered if the pony had been ridden very much.

"Come on, Jamie. Just a little ride," Kate pleaded with him.

"But the Métis could come back at any time."

"Just put me on his back to see what it's like."

"We don't have a bridle, let alone a saddle. You can't control a horse if you don't have a bit in its mouth."

"You can do something," Kate pleaded with him. She wanted to ride this horse more than anything else in the world.

"There is the rope that hobbles his front legs," said Jamie. "I wonder …" He patted the horse's neck and chest to let him get the smell of him. "Maybe I could get the rope between his teeth and use it as a bit."

"Could we ride him then?"

"Just a short ride around here. Then we'll hobble him again. But you've got to promise not to tell anyone."

"I promise, Jamie. No one will know. Not Meg or Mother or even Robbie."

"All right," Jamie said, running his hand down the horse's front leg and beginning to undo the rope that hobbled his two legs together. The knots had pulled tight and were difficult to loosen, but finally they came apart, and the rope was in his hands.

The horse stood rigid and trembling. Jamie spoke quietly. "Easy, boy ... easy. There's a good pony."

When the horse had quieted, Jamie explained, "You're going to get on his back first, Kate. Grab hold of his mane. I'll come up behind you."

"Do I sit sidesaddle?"

"You're not one of those English ladies. You'll have to straddle him and hold on with your knees."

"I've got this long skirt."

"You wanted to ride, didn't you? Come on. Up you go."

A couple of times, Kate tried to pull herself onto the horse's back, but it was too high, and the horse shied away. He would have bolted completely if Jamie had not held onto his neck.

"You'll have to climb up on me and then boost yourself onto his back, Kate."

She climbed up onto Jamie's knee and then lay across the pony's back. Grabbing the thick mane, Kate managed to swing her legs around so that she was straddling the horse. All the time he danced and whinnied nervously. When he calmed, she pulled her skirt until it settled around her legs, and she could grip the flanks of the horse.

Jamie spoke quietly to the nervous animal. He held the rope up to his mouth, but the horse clamped his teeth together and would not open. The boy pushed and pried against the steely jaws until the pony finally opened enough to let the rope slip into his mouth.

"Here, Kate. Hold onto the ends of the rope until I get up," Jamie said, handing the rope to her and moving along the side of the horse. "That a boy ... easy, boy ..." He positioned himself beside the pony, grasped Kate around the waist, and then leapt up behind her in one bound. Quickly he reached around on either side of his sister and took the reins from her.

The horse stood trembling. Jamie squeezed his knees together to hold on. At any moment he expected the pony to buck and kick in an effort to get rid of them, but the animal did nothing but stand stiff and still.

"Come on. Let's go for a ride," Kate said, but nothing happened. "What's wrong, Jamie?"

"Maybe he's never been trained."

"Make him go, please."

Gently the boy nudged the pony's ribs with his heels. Instantly the horse began to move, first in a trot and then a gallop. The two of them moved with the rhythm of the pounding hooves.

Kate shrieked happily. She loved the feeling of movement, the rush of the wind through her hair, and the sense of the galloping horse beneath her.

But the pony was heading in the direction of their camp. Jamie pulled the reins, trying to steer him back toward the pasture they had come from, but he would not change direction. They were galloping even faster now.

They could see Meg digging at the house site. She dropped her shovel and shouted, but they could not hear what she said. "What's Mother going to say?" Kate shouted above the pounding hooves.

Jamie was fighting with the horse, trying to bring him under control. The pony had the rope clamped between his teeth and did not respond to the hard tugs and pulls on the reins. The tan and black horse was in a full racing gallop now, running at top speed across the bald prairie.

"Jamie! He's going too fast! Slow him down!" Kate shouted.

"I can't!"

"Make him stop! Please, Jamie!"

But there was no way he could control the horse now. He was galloping at full speed toward the trees that lined the

Assiniboine River, running ever faster now, leaning his neck forward, racing with all his power to some imagined goal. Everything was a blur of motion. It was all Jamie could do to keep himself and his sister on the horse's back.

The boy did not see the others until they were upon them. Suddenly there was one horse on either side of them, racing as fast as their pony. He could feel the flanks of the other horses squeezing them from either side. A hand reached forward, grasped the reins from him, and yanked hard. The three horses lurched to a stop together.

Jamie was panting hard with the effort. It took him a moment to collect himself. He checked to see that Kate was all right and then looked around. On one side was a heavyset, middle-aged man with a full beard, on the other was the young Métis they had argued with the day before.

They had saved them, maybe spared their lives.

# 4

"M*on Dieu!*" the bearded man declared.

"What are you doing?" The younger Métis man was annoyed and angry. "Ride the horse without a bridle. Stupid. Could kill yourself."

The older man said something in a language neither Kate nor Jamie could understand. The younger one translated. "My father, he says this is a buffalo pony. Very fast, very, how do you say, very high-spirited." He spoke good English but with a heavy accent.

The horse had calmed down. He had played himself out in the frantic run and now was covered in a heavy wet lather.

Kate had finally recovered from the fright. "I don't know what to say. We took your horse without asking and then you had to risk yourself to save us."

Jamie felt sheepish. "It was a really stupid thing to do."

The two men talked among themselves for a moment. Kate was sure that she understood some of what they were saying. *"Parlez-vous français?"* she asked.

*"Mais oui,"* replied the older man with a big smile lighting his face. *"Vous parlez français aussi, ma fille?"*

*"Oui ..."* Kate and Jamie and the others in the Bains family had been brought up in a French district of Ottawa and had spoken French with friends and neighbours. Jamie had been away and his second language was rusty, but Kate spoke it fluently. "But I didn't understand everything you were saying," she added in French.

"We speak Red River dialect," the man explained in excellent French. "It's a mixture of French and Cree — just like the Métis people ourselves. I learned to speak French in school at St. Boniface, many years ago, but I do not speak English."

The young man was obviously upset. "These are the people I was telling you about, Father," he said in French. "They are settling on our pasture lands."

"Times are changing Louis ... the buffalo and now the settlers ... But these are new people to the prairie, and we must welcome them."

"No! It's not fair. Soon the Métis will have nothing."

"Ride home, Louis. Get a bridle and saddle. If these young people are to ride a horse, they must have the right gear."

"No Father. It's not fair, I tell you! Why did we stand with Louis Riel if it all comes to this?"

"The Métis who ignores the needs of the stranger, in our land, is not a man at all. Go! Bring the bridle and saddle."

Louis glared at his father for a moment. Then he dug his heels into the sides of his bay horse. The animal broke into a gallop, and they rode toward the trees.

The father slipped off his horse to the ground. He was wearing a cloth shirt with buckskin trousers and beautifully hand-stitched moccasins. Around his waist was a long red sash. He was a short man, heavyset and powerful. He spoke French in a formal, educated way that Kate found strange in a man who lived on the frontier.

"You will have to excuse Louis," he explained. "He's a hot-tempered man like many of the Dauphin family. I was known to be like that myself when I was young. Come. I'll tell you about this animal that you've been riding."

Jamie slid off the back of the horse and Kate let herself be lifted down by Monsieur Dauphin.

"This is a special horse, bred for the buffalo hunt. I rode on his father seven summers in a row. He could cut out a big bull buffalo and hold to its side until I could bring him down. Such courage that horse. Like a lion. I've never seen the likes of it in all my years on the hunt."

Kate was listening to every word of the buffalo hunter. Jamie found that he could understand most of what was being said. Dauphin was an expressive, warm man who loved to talk.

"After the father got too old I was going to ride this horse on the hunt, only the buffalo have faded into the prairie. In the last three seasons, they have disappeared — turned into bones and dust."

"What happened to them?" Kate asked in French.

He shrugged expressively and said, "Maybe they've gone west into the Blackfoot country of the foothills. Maybe north among the caribou. Some say they have been hunted out, but there were so many of them how can that be possible? With my own eyes, I have seen herds of thousands of buffalo — hundreds of thousands — so many that they blackened the prairie as far as the eye could see. How can they all be gone?"

He paused to pat the tan and black pony. "Ah, his father was a magnificent horse and this one would have been the match for him. Fast and strong and intelligent and fearless, that's what you need in a buffalo pony. This would have been one of the best."

"Why does he have such pretty markings?" Kate asked.

"His father was a tan colour and his mother was black with long legs and a strong neck. She was a racer — as fast as the wind. When we were chasing you, we could barely catch up. That speed comes from the mother."

They talked on, or rather Monsieur Dauphin talked on, until Louis came back onto the prairie, carrying a bridle and saddle. He rode up and threw them on the ground, making it clear that he was still annoyed.

Jamie picked up the bridle. It was worn but still in reasonably good condition. "Should I put it on?" he asked in broken French.

"Ah, you speak a little of the language yourself, boy? Yes, saddle him up. Let's see what you know about horses."

Jamie was happy to comply. He had spent months working as a stable boy and knew more about saddling horses than he cared to remember. He made some adjustments to the bridle and pulled it over the horse's head. Getting the bit into his mouth was a problem, but the pony finally relented and let the piece of steel slip between his teeth.

"You've got to remember that all horses are the same," Dauphin said. "You've got to show them who's in control. You have to be confident and strong and decisive. If they think you don't know what you're doing, they'll lead you on a merry chase." He inspected Jamie's work. "It looks good, lad. You know what you're doing. I can see that." The boy warmed to the praise. "Now saddle him up."

It took only a moment to spread the blanket on the pony's back, throw up the saddle, and pull the cinch tight.

"Who's going to take him for a ride first?" Dauphin asked, looking at the two of them. "What's your name, lad?"

"Jamie."

"Strange name that, Jamie." He repeated the name to himself. "And you, young miss, what is your name?"

"Kathleen. Kate is what the family calls me."

"Kate." He pronounced it in a guttural way and then laughed at himself. "That's too hard for a French tongue. Kat'leen. That is what we will call you. Kat'leen the rider of the wild horses," and he laughed again. "All right, lad … Jamie. Let's see you ride this buffalo pony."

Jamie took a minute to adjust the stirrups. He stood on the left side of the horse, patted his neck, and whispered gently into his ear. "That a boy. Going to go for a little ride. Nice and easy."

He put his foot into the stirrup and swung himself into the saddle. The pony bolted a few steps. Jamie pulled hard on the reins. The horse fought against the bit, but the boy held firm, and the animal came to a stop.

"Easy now ... easy," Jamie whispered into the horse's ear. "Come on. Just an easy run. Let's show them what we can do." The boy nudged him with his heels, and the horse moved into a trot. Jamie gave him his head for a minute, letting him lope along at his own speed across the prairie. Then he turned him to the left, and the horse instantly responded to the command.

The boy and the horse worked together. Jamie nudged him with his heels again, and the horse broke into a faster trot. He turned him to the right, and then to the left, and each time the pony responded immediately. He nudged him again and they were in a gallop, then pulled back on the reins and he slowed. The horse and the rider had become one, in a smooth, fluid movement. Finally Jamie steered the pony back to the spot where the others were standing and brought him to a halt.

"*Très bien*," said the older Dauphin. "You know how to ride a horse, lad. Ride like that and you might be welcomed on the buffalo hunt some day."

"Monsieur Dauphin, we have to get back to the camp," said Kate in French. "Our mother will be worried."

"*Mais oui*. We had best come with you to explain. Let's go," Dauphin replied swinging up onto his mount. "Come, Kat'leen. You can ride up behind me."

He reached his hand down to Kate. She grasped it, and he lifted her onto the horse's back with one easy movement. She sat behind him, holding onto his waist.

"Come, Louis," Dauphin ordered.

"I'm not going."

"It's to pay a social call on new neighbours. It's only polite."

"I won't have anything to do with these English who come to take up our land."

Dauphin was upset with Louis. "I'll not have a son of mine treat strangers as if they are not welcome on this land!"

Louis glared at his father, but he climbed on his horse, and the three animals and their riders rode toward the camp in the distance.

When they came to the camp, they found Peggy Bains so worried and upset her reaction at seeing them was a confused mixture of relief and anger. She was still wearing the work clothes she had put on for ploughing. Her face was smeared with dirt.

"Oh, my God, I thought … I thought something horrible had happened." Kate slipped to the ground and rushed to give her mother a hug. "Who's horse is that, Jamie? What's the meaning of this?" she demanded.

The boy felt sheepish. "It belongs to Monsieur Dauphin, here," he said in awkward French.

"You took his horse without permission?" she continued in English. "This is terrible, Jamie. You should be ashamed of yourself. Anything could have happened. An accident. Kate could have been thrown off." She put her hands to her face and tears welled up in her eyes. "I thought you were never coming back … I …"

Kate and Meg tried to console their mother. She began to cry from the sheer relief of seeing her children again. Robbie stroked his mother's back, upset to see her crying.

Jamie slipped off the horse and stood in front of Peggy with the reins in his hands. "I'm sorry, Mother," he muttered.

"You shouldn't blame Jamie," said Kate, close to tears herself. "It's my fault. I begged him to take me for a ride on the horse."

"Then you both deserve to be punished," Peggy replied. Suddenly she seemed to realize that they had company. "I'm sorry," she said breaking away from the ring created by her children and approaching the bearded man still sitting on his horse. "I'm sorry. I'm so rude. It's just that I am so relieved."

"He only speaks French," Kate explained. "Monsieur Dauphin is his name."

"*Monsieur Dauphin, comment ça va? Je suis Peggy Bains*. I have to apologize for my children and for myself," she continued in French. "It's just that I was so worried."

"Not at all, Madam Bains. I understand perfectly. I must apologize as well for it was my horse. Had he not been there, the temptation would not have existed." He spoke in a formal, proper manner.

"It was wrong for them to take him."

"It is the nature of children to seek adventure and ride on the prairie. I have been known to do it myself," he added, then chuckled. "My wife says that I am still a foolish man, riding the prairies for no more reason than to feel a horse beneath me and the sky above."

"You are most generous." Then she turned to her children but continued speaking in French. "Jamie, Kate, the least you can do is make us all a pot of tea for all the trouble and heartache that you've caused us." Then she turned back to their guest. "You will stay for a cup, Monsieur Dauphin?"

Peggy and her family had known French people all of their lives. They loved their *joie de vivre*, and the warmth and affection they showed toward their friends. Dauphin's outgoing personality made them like him immediately.

"It is true that the Métis have always enjoyed a cup of tea," Dauphin continued. "That's one thing the English from the Hudson's Bay Company taught us." He slid off his horse, and the group made its way to the campfire. Jamie and Kate rushed ahead to get things ready. They were eager to make amends for all the trouble they had caused.

"I think you have met my son Louis," Dauphin said. "He's my oldest. I've got another five at home."

Louis had climbed off his horse and stood quietly with his reins in his hands. His slim Indian features gave him an athletic, strong look. He was watchful and sullen, a stark contrast to his father's talkative, outgoing cheerfulness. As he stood on the outskirts of the group, Louis stole a quick look at Meg. She glanced up and for an instance their eyes met. Both of them quickly looked away.

"We met the day we arrived. He ..." Peggy stopped for a moment. "He seemed angry that we had taken a homestead on this land."

Louis looked at Peggy and then at her daughter Meg. "This is Métis land," he said in French in a low, threatening voice. "They have no right to give it away to English from Ontario."

"But you were given other land that you can farm," said Meg.

"That's true. Métis were given prairie land, but it is far away. This has always been the pasture land for the Dauphin family," Louis replied, looking arrogantly at the young woman.

"But this can be much more than just pasture land," Meg argued. "It can produce wheat or vegetables and who knows what else?"

"But it is our land. Don't you understand?"

"Louis, hold your tongue!" demanded Dauphin.

"You're just like all the others, Father! Soon we'll have no pasture land. There will be no buffalo, no cart trains to take across the prairies. All that will be left for the Métis people will be little strip farms along the river that can support no more than an old man and an old woman. I can't stand the thought of it."

Louis swept onto his bay horse in one easy movement. Looking one last time at Meg, he hit his horse on the flank with his hat. It leapt into a gallop, and he rode south onto the wide open prairie, where he could be alone under the blue expanse of sky.

"That lad will come to harm if he carries on like this," said Dauphin as he watched his son ride away.

Kate and Jamie had a good fire under the pot of water when the others came to the campfire. Dauphin, Meg, and Peggy sat on boxes while the three younger kids listened to them talk as they sat on the ground. The conversation was in French, and though the members of the Bains family had different skills in the language, they could all understand and participate.

The talk was about the Métis people, and the life of the Bains family before they came to Manitoba, and then Dauphin asked Peggy in his blunt, straightforward manner. "How are you to survive on your farm out here on the prairie? Now it is warm. The sun shines, and the land is good to us, but winter will soon arrive. For six months we are locked in a deep freeze. The blizzards blow for days, and you can barely get out of your house. There is no food, the birds have gone." He shook his head and added, "You have to be prepared or the family will starve."

Peggy was almost afraid to talk about it. "The truth is, Monsieur Dauphin, our money is almost gone. I have to get the ploughing finished so that we can plant our crop. We're surviving on little more than bannock and porridge." She was not sure that she should be speaking about her worries, especially in front of the children, but it was reassuring to talk to another adult.

"Humm ... problem, problem ..." Dauphin stroked his beard and sipped his black tea. "Then it's up to these young people, isn't it?" He pointed to Robbie, Kate, and Jamie sitting on the grass and smiled. "You'll have to learn to live off the land. And in the fall, when there is real plenty ... Well, we'll talk about that when the time comes."

He got to his feet. "I have to go now. The wife and children will be wondering where this old prairie wanderer has taken himself. Bad enough to have one in the family out riding in all directions."

He climbed aboard his mount. "*Merci, monsieur Dauphin.* Thank you for everything," said Peggy.

Kate held the bridle of his horse for a moment. "And we apologize again, sir."

"*Ah ... ma fille.* You like that horse so much. It's yours. It's for you and your brothers. Care for him well and ride him like the wind," he said, laughing as he rode away.

Kate was shocked at the generosity. It was all she could do to shout her thanks after him. *"Merci, Monsieur Dauphin! Merci, merci, merci!"*

# 5

Kate and Jamie could barely believe their good fortune. "He's really ours," Kate repeated, "our very own horse."

Jamie went over to the animal tethered by the cart. It was hard to believe that he was theirs.

"And Monsieur Dauphin gave him to me, too," said Robbie. "Will you teach me how to ride, Jamie?"

Their mother tried to bring them down to earth. "He is such a generous man, but we've got to get back to work. We have already wasted enough of this day what with riding horses across the prairie. I've got the ploughing to do and the rest of you have to dig the hole for the house."

"Can we just take him for a little ride?" begged Kate.

"We have to work," Peggy said with a touch of annoyance. "Kate, you don't seem to understand. Our survival depends on getting the planting done and finishing the house." But when she saw the disappointment in her daughter's face, she added, "All right, maybe after supper you can ride him for a while."

They left the horse saddled and ready to ride and went to the hole they were digging for the house while their mother resumed ploughing. Meg and Jamie took turns digging. It was hard work. The sod had been stripped off, and they were digging in bare dirt, but the earth was filled with small roots from the wild grass that went deep into the ground. The dark loam was moist and heavy.

Jamie worked extra hard because he felt guilty for having snuck away and ridden the horse. Soon he was sweating from the effort and covered in dirt, but he kept at it without a break.

They worked until they saw their mother walking wearily back from the fields. The others helped to ease her into one of the makeshift chairs in the camp.

"Jamie, will you be a dear and go and look after Baby?" she asked. "I just didn't have the strength."

Meg was very concerned. "You can't continue working this hard, Mother."

"I've got to get this ploughing done, Meg. We only have a few days to get the wheat planted or it will never ripen in time."

"But you're exhausted."

"It's just the stiffness in my muscles. I'll get used to it. Just let me rest for a bit."

Jamie and Kate went to the field, unshackled Baby from the plough, took off his yoke, and set him free to range in the long grass. They did not have to hobble him. An ox never wandered very far. When they got back to the camp, Meg was preparing supper, and their mother was asleep.

Robbie came running up. "Can we ride him now? Mum said we could ride at supper time."

Meg smiled and nodded at her younger brother, and the boy ran back to the others, filled with excitement. Jamie got the buffalo pony and led him away from the camp. "I'm going to teach Kate how to ride first. Then I'll teach you, Robbie."

Their younger brother was disappointed, but he sat on the grass and watched the lesson.

Jamie led the buffalo pony a distance away from the camp while he talked to his younger sister. "It's important that a horse gets to know you. Let him smell you and listen to your voice. Then he won't be so frightened and hard to handle. If you're kind, a horse will work with you. If you treat him badly, he'll always be trouble."

Kate smiled. "They're just like people."

"I guess. Now, stand here on his left side, Kate. You always mount a horse from the left. Up you go."

Kate swung easily into the saddle. "This long skirt gets in the way," she said as she settled.

"Sit up straight in the saddle. That's right. Hold the reins in front of you. Good."

Jamie stepped back from the horse. The tan and black pony watched him nervously with wide frightened eyes. For a moment the boy thought the horse might bolt, but he grew calm and stood stock-still, looking at them as if waiting for instructions.

"Hold the reins in tight until you want him to move. Don't forget to hold onto his sides with your knees. Let the reins out a little and give him a little nudge with your heels."

Miraculously the pony began to move in an easy trot. "Good, Kate, perfect. Work with him. Now bring him to a stop."

But the pony did not slow. "Make him stop!" Jamie ordered.

"I'm trying, Jamie! He won't stop!"

Jamie panicked. What if he bolted again? "Harder, Kate! Make him feel that you're in command!"

She yanked on the reins. The horse's head jerked up, and he came to an abrupt halt. Jamie ran over with a sense of relief and grasped the halter.

"You did it, Kate!"

She beamed from the praise. "You really think I can ride him, Jamie?"

"You're going to be a good rider! I can tell."

They stopped the lesson long enough to eat a hurried supper and then came back to ride again. Jamie got up on the pony and showed Kate how to handle the reins and how to steer him. Then she got onto the horse and trotted about practising until she became bored.

"I want to take him for a gallop," she called out.

"You're not ready yet." But it turned out that it was not Jamie's decision.

Kate suddenly nudged the horse sharply in the side. "Come on pony … Get up there!" She raised herself up on the stirrups and began to move. "Let's go!"

"No, Kate, don't!"

But the young girl ignored her brother. The horse broke into a run and then into a hard gallop. Kate was moving with the rhythm of the animal, using the motion of her body to respond to the motion of the horse.

Jamie stood beside Robbie, staring after her. He was afraid and yet filled with admiration at the daring of his young sister. She had an independent spirit, and no one was going to tell her what to do.

Kate rode into the prairie, galloping with all the speed of the buffalo pony, until they were a long way away. Then she pulled on the reins, and the horse responded immediately to her directions. They turned and headed back to the camp in an easy trot. The last hundred yards she urged the pony into a gallop again and brought him back to her two brothers with a rush and a flourish.

"For someone who was never on the back of a horse until a few hours ago that was some ride," said Jamie with a smile.

Kate beamed with the praise of her older brother.

It was a full evening. Robbie wanted a ride, and they began his lesson by putting him on the back of the horse, with Kate leading him on foot.

"Let me ride by myself," Robbie pleaded.

"You will soon enough," answered Jamie. "First, just get the feel of the horse and move with him. That's how Kate was able to learn so fast."

When they were finished, the sun was beginning to set. Golds and reds and yellows streaked the western sky in a spectacular display.

They took off the saddle and bridle, then tied a loose hobble on the pony's front legs so that he could range on the grasslands and not get far away. Then the three of them joined their mother and sister around the campfire.

"We are fortunate," said Peggy quietly. "Monsieur Dauphin is so generous. I was wondering, Jamie. Do you think that you could build some type of sled that your pony could pull?"

"Sled? What do you mean?"

"We don't have any wheels to make a wagon, but if we could build some rig that the horse could pull, then we can use him to haul things."

"He's not a workhorse, Mother," Jamie replied, incensed. "He's a riding horse."

"Everyone around here has to work. Horses, oxen, everyone."

"He's a buffalo pony and bred for the hunt."

"I'm too tired to argue, but think about it. A sled of some sort for hauling things, it wouldn't be so terrible."

As they climbed into bed, the black flies and mosquitoes began to swarm around their heads. Peggy was too exhausted to notice. Her back and arms were so stiff from wrestling with the plough that she could barely crawl under the blankets.

"You can't continue working this hard, Mother," Meg said as she settled into the blankets, but her mother was already asleep.

It was an awful night. The black flies swarmed in among them, and when they woke in the morning, they were all bitten on their faces and hands. Robbie was in the worst shape of all. His face was swollen from the bites, and there was blood crusted along his hairline and behind his ears.

His mother took him down to the stream to wash the blood away. She was worried about Robbie. He had never been strong, and Peggy feared that this rugged life might be too much for him.

John, her oldest son, had been like that when he was young — delicate and tender. He was always daydreaming or had his head buried in a book. Work in the logging camp had changed him, and she wondered if Robbie would change as well.

Peggy missed John almost as much as she missed her husband. Often she wondered if she would ever see him again.

The day started with porridge and then the work began. Already the Bains kids were getting restless. Was this never going to stop?

Their mother dressed in her ploughing gear again and went down to the field to continue the tedious task of turning the furrows. Kate and Robbie tidied up the camp while Jamie and Meg went back to digging the hole for the house. It was discouraging. Even though they worked endlessly, the hole seemed no deeper than before.

They worked as best they could. Taking turns, one of them would dig up a shovelful, walk to the outside of the house, dump it and then come back and give the shovel to the other. They had been at it for hours, and the end was nowhere in sight.

By mid-morning Jamie needed a break, and when Meg suggested they go down to check on their mother, he jumped at the chance. The two younger kids joined them, and they walked together toward the field.

It was another lovely day. The bright sunshine was beating down, and a light breeze stirred the grass. Robbie pointed out a big eagle circling in the sky, searching for prey. He noticed the natural life on the prairie more than the others.

Meg was worried. "Mother's pushing herself too hard. We've got to do something."

"She won't listen, Meg," said Kate.

"I know. What can we do?" but no one had an answer.

Their mother was at the other end of the field, wrestling with the handles of the plough as Baby plodded on. They stood and watched until she finished the furrow and then they insisted that she take a break. She stretched as she walked away from the plough. The muscles in her arms and back were so stiff and sore they ached constantly.

"Let me do some ploughing for a while," suggested Jamie.

"I don't think you have the strength."

"I'm as big and as strong as you are," he replied, feeling a little insulted by her comment. After all, he was fourteen and had been working for more than a year now.

"Let him try," said Meg.

Jamie did not wait for an answer. He positioned Baby so that he was heading down the next furrow and pulled and tugged at the heavy plough until it was in place.

"Come on Baby. Let's go," he said, touching him with the prodding stick. The big ox began lumbering down the field. Jamie shifted his weight onto the handles. The plough blade sunk into the earth, and a neat furrow curled back exposing the rich black soil.

The handles bucked and twisted as the plough ran into resistance. The boy soon grew tired as he wrestled with them trying to keep the furrow straight, but he was not about to give up. He liked the smell of the fresh-turned earth and the warmth of the soil. Jamie did not even notice that the others had gone back to the camp. He finished one furrow, then turned Baby and the plough and immediately headed back in the same direction.

As he ploughed, Jamie thought about his mother's idea of a sled for the buffalo pony. Maybe it wasn't such a bad idea. They would use the horse mainly for riding, but what was wrong with him doing a few chores? As his mother had said, everyone had to work in this family.

But how to attach the sled? They did not have the collar used when a horse pulled a load. The shafts would have to be attached to the saddle in some way. How would he do it so they did not rub against the horse's flanks?

He found the problem interesting to think about, and it helped pass the time. Almost before he knew it, Robbie had arrived and was calling him for lunch.

After eating, their mother went back on the plough again, and Jamie and Meg returned to the hated job of digging the hole for the house. They had worked no more than ten minutes when they heard the sound of a horse. They looked up and found Louis Dauphin sitting on his bay pony not fifteen paces away, watching them. It gave them both a sudden start.

"Why are you digging the hole?" Louis asked in English. The anger he had shown the last time they met had disappeared.

"It's for our house," Meg explained. For a moment she felt awkward and uncertain of herself with Louis, but she smiled and pushed her hair back, leaving a smudge of dirt on her face.

"Sure could take a long time." He slid off his pony and stood at the edge of the hole, and Meg came to stand beside him.

She felt a strange excitement to be so close to the young Métis. Before he had seemed so hostile — angry at their very presence — but now he smiled at her shyly, and his dark eyes betrayed his interest.

"It would be faster if we had some help," Meg replied, smiling coyly. She was surprised at herself for being so bold.

Louis hesitated for a moment. "You mean ..." but he left the rest unsaid.

"If you want ..." Meg shrugged but watched him intently.

He laughed and said, "But I am wearing moccasins not boots." Then he laughed again, stepped into the hole, and took the shovel from Meg's hands. "How much dirt do you want out of here?"

Jamie slipped out of the pit without being noticed. Kate caught her brother's eye. She smirked and nodded at the couple. Jamie sniggered in return.

"Let's give these love birds some privacy," Jamie said. "Come on! Let's go riding!"

The two scouted out on the prairie until they found the buffalo pony. It did not take long to catch him and saddle up.

"Let's go down to the river to see if we can find some poles to build a sled for the pony," Jamie suggested.

"I thought you didn't want to do that."

"Let's go and see."

They both climbed aboard the horse, Jamie in the saddle and Kate holding on behind, and rode over to the camp to fetch the axe. When Robbie found out they were going riding, he begged to come with them.

"Three is a lot for the horse," Jamie said.

But Robbie would not relent and finally Jamie agreed. The three of them climbed up onto the pony with Jamie in the saddle, Robbie sitting in front of him holding onto the mane, and Kate behind. The horse loped across the prairie with an easy movement as if he enjoyed the effort.

They were close to the line of trees that boarded the Assiniboine River when they came across a marshy area created by the creek. There were bulrushes and wild rice plants. Robbie spotted a flock of ducks swimming on the pond. He was very interested in birds of all types and wanted to have a closer look.

Jamie brought the horse to a stop and let the boy slide down to the ground. "Kate and I are going to find some poles for our sled," Jamie explained. "Don't go near the water, Robbie." The boy waved and disappeared into some bulrushes before they had ridden five paces.

They rode to the very edge of the trees, tied up the buffalo pony, and, taking the axe, began exploring. The grade down to the river was quite steep and covered with poplar trees of all sizes.

"I figure we need two fairly long pieces for the shafts and then a bunch of shorter pieces for the sled," Jamie explained.

"Why can't we let the pony pull the cart?" Kate asked.

"It's too big, and it's designed to be pulled with the yoke made to fit the ox. It's better that we make something for the pony."

They had walked part way down the hill when Kate pointed through the trees. "Look, Jamie." Off in the distance they could see a clearing with a log house, stables, and a big garden. Beyond that were other strip farms coming back from the river.

"It's the Métis settlement," said Jamie. "That must be where Monsieur Dauphin and his family live."

But they had no time to visit. They found a couple of long poplar trees the right size for the shafts, cut them down, trimmed off the branches, and dragged them back to where their horse was tethered. Then they cut down a much bigger tree, chopped it into three pieces, and wrestled all three back to the wood stack.

Jamie and Kate talked about how they were going to get the wood back to camp, but they had no rope or wagon. Finally they decided to leave it and come back for it later.

When they rode toward the marsh, they found Robbie running in their direction. At first they thought something was wrong. Jamie urged the pony into a gallop and raced toward him, but as they got closer they saw that their brother was pointing to something he had wrapped up in a big cloth.

"Eggs," he said excitedly. "Duck eggs. I found lots of them."

They reined in the horse and climbed down. Sure enough Robbie had collected a dozen or more small speckled brown eggs.

"Oh, look, one of them is broken," said the boy with disappointment.

"That doesn't matter. You've got lots," said Kate.

"Do you think Mum will be pleased?"

"She'll be overjoyed."

They rode back to the camp and called their mother and Meg to come and see. Peggy could barely believe their good fortune. She hugged her youngest child. "This is wonderful, Robbie! Wonderful! We're going to have the biggest feed. We're all so hungry!"

Even Louis was impressed. "There are lots of ducks, and this is the time of year they are laying eggs, but it's hard to find the nests."

They stopped work, Jamie started a fire, and Louis stayed to eat a big meal of bannock and scrambled eggs. After they finished, they sat around the fire talking and enjoying the warmth of the day. Kate spotted two men riding toward their camp on big workhorses. It was Mr. Campbell along with a younger man. Both were dressed in farmer's work clothes.

"Evenin'," said Campbell as he rode up. He nodded to the others as they exchanged pleasantries.

"You're just in time for a cup of tea," offered Peggy. "Will you join us?"

"Don't mind if we do," replied Campbell, and he and the younger man climbed off their horses. As they settled around the fire, he continued, "Thought I would bring over our new neighbour for introductions. This here is Albert Marshall, a bachelor who has taken a homestead about a mile west of my place."

Albert was in his early twenties, not much older than Louis. He was a short, clean-shaven man with square, powerful shoulders. The young farmer glanced uneasily at Louis, and then smiled warmly at Meg and shook her hand.

Louis looked uneasily from Albert and Campbell and back to Meg again. He was obviously uncomfortable with the two men.

"Are there any other settlers?" asked Peggy casually.

"Lots of them are comin'," Albert replied, positioning himself beside Meg. "I was in Winnipeg just three days ago, and the land registry office was bulging at the seams with people comin' in to take homesteads." He smiled at the prospect. "All good Orange, Protestant folk from Ontario. The best people on God's good earth. They're gonna make thousands of prosperous farms out here on the prairie."

Louis stiffened. "They are coming to take Métis land," he said in his heavy accent.

Albert looked annoyed and replied, "They're settlers. Homesteaders. They're gonna fill up this land."

"Then how are the Métis to live!" Louis was enraged.

"The land was given by the government," Albert said defensively.

"The buffalo have gone. Once this land is farmed, all the wild game will disappear. You and your settlers will destroy the Métis people!"

"You have your own land down by the river!" Now Albert was shouting. "Stay on it or there will be trouble!"

"Please, no more of this!" demanded Peggy.

Louis would not stay and listen to any more. He untied his horse and climbed into the saddle. "Let me tell you something!" he said, pointing directly at Albert. "This is Métis land, and it's going to stay Métis land!" He kicked his horse, and his pony galloped out of the camp toward the settlements along the river.

Campbell shook his head as he watched him go. "He's trouble. Real trouble if you ask me."

Albert was still furious. "What right does he have to tell us that we can't take homesteads? He has to be taught a lesson."

"He's young," replied Peggy, trying to defuse the conflict.

Campbell was shaking his head. "He's stirrin' up the Métis. That's what worries me. He's gettin' them so that they're all going to hate the English Canadians. Maybe we'll be facin' rebellion again."

The tea was made now, and they settled around the fire to drink it. They chatted for a while, and then Mr. Campbell told them why he had come to visit. "We want you and the whole family over to our place on Sunday for a visit, Mrs. Bains, so you can get to meet the neighbours. Seems to me we should talk about this business with the Métis, as well."

"That's for certain," said Albert emphatically.

Peggy stirred uneasily. "I'm not so sure I want to leave the farm until we have finished planting."

"We're going to gather on Sunday afternoon. No one works on Sundays in these parts. You can meet Ruby, my missus. Give you the chance to talk women talk."

"I'll try, Mr. Campbell, but I can't guarantee it."

# 6

Once Mr. Campbell and Albert had left, Meg let her true feelings be known. "I'm not going to gossip about our neighbours."

"Are you afraid they're going to talk about Louis?" Kate asked with a smirk.

Meg turned on her sister. "How would you like it if people talked about us behind our back, Kate? They're busy-bodies condemning other people because they're different."

"Maybe that's why we need to go," said Peggy thoughtfully.

"What do you mean?"

"If we're there, we can find out what they're planning."

"They might have some kids our age," added Robbie.

"Well, I'm not going," Meg shot back decisively. "They're nothing but a bunch of hypocrites." She turned away from the others and busied herself by collecting the supper dishes.

It was still early, so Peggy went back to the field to plough more furrows. Meg and the two younger kids worked around the camp. Robbie and Kate were given the chore of scrubbing out the supper dishes in the creek with sand while Meg prepared the beds and tidied up.

Jamie was anxious to get working on the sled. He found a long rope in the cart and rode off on the buffalo pony to collect the logs that they had cut earlier that afternoon.

It was a beautiful ride. As the sun slowly sank in the west, the shadows lengthened, giving a softness to the landscape.

Jamie moved with the easy rhythm of the pony's canter, watching the scene slowly unfold around him.

Wildlife of all kinds scattered as they rode across the prairie. A family of grouse flew up out of the long grass. A prairie chicken ran away, frightened by the hooves of the pony. Jamie spotted several rabbits running for cover, and he thought he saw a badger sneaking through the grass. As they passed close by the marsh, a dozen ducks took off across the pond, their wings beating on the water until they were airborne. Close to the line of trees, two white-tailed deer bounded across the landscape and found cover in the underbrush.

As he neared the edge of the trees, he suddenly spotted a group of Indians a long distance to the west. It looked like they were on the trail leading to the ford over the river. There were seven or eight of them, women, men, and children, all on horseback, pulling long travois attached to their ponies.

For a moment the boy felt a sense of panic. His family would be defenceless against attack. To the south the Sioux Indians were still at war against the U.S. army, but his family had been told the Indians in these parts were friendly. He watched the Indian band until he was satisfied there was nothing to worry about and then went back to the business at hand.

Jamie found the long poles and logs without any trouble. He got off the pony, bundled the wood together, and tied the rope securely around it with three hitches. Then he secured the other end of the rope by tying it onto a ring on the saddle.

At first he walked on foot, leading the pony with the reins in his hands and dragging the poles behind them. It was a problem. The poles kept catching in the long grass, and he had to go back and free them before they could start again. Finally he was able to rig it up so that the rope held the ends of the poles up, and they snaked along behind them. After walking like this for a while, Jamie climbed back up on the pony, and they rode across the prairie.

It was remarkable how well the horse pulled the load, the boy thought. Just a couple of days before, he had been a wild range pony. Now he was responding to every command.

When Jamie got back to the camp, the light was failing as the sun set. Peggy was just returning from the field. A small campfire gave a warm soft light. The place was beginning to feel like home.

Jamie untied the load, took off the saddle, hobbled the pony, and turned him loose. When he walked to the camp, he heard Meg explaining to their mother.

"When we were working on the house, Louis told me that if you set the grass on fire, especially the green grass, it makes a smoke or smudge that keeps the bugs away."

Kate and Robbie each took a big bundle of grass they had prepared and put one end in the fire. Soon it began to give off billowy clouds of white smoke. They waved it all around until the whole campsite was filled with the sweet, fresh smell of burning grass.

"That's good, Meg," said their mother. "I don't think we could live another night with those swarming bugs."

It was not perfect. The black flies and mosquitoes buzzed around most of the night, but it was better than the night before, and in the morning they had fewer bites.

Peggy felt better that morning. She was getting used to the heavy work of ploughing and was not nearly as exhausted. She went out into the fields with more optimism than she had felt since she had started.

Jamie was determined to begin work on the sled. He could now see that this would save them a lot of work, and the sooner it was completed the better. Kate and Robbie helped him as best they could, but he planned it out by himself.

The real difficulty was the shortage of tools and supplies. They had no nails, but they did have a hand drill and lots of rope and heavy cord. It was going to be tricky, but with a little ingenuity, he thought he could build something that would stand up for at least one season.

With dogged determination, Meg stayed at the chore of digging the hole for the house. It was the most boring and unpleasant of jobs, but as soon as breakfast was over, she got out the shovel and went off without complaint. She had been working for little more than an hour when she heard the sound of a horse and looked up to find Louis.

He smiled at her and held up a pair of boots and a shovel. "This time I come prepared," he said in English. Soon the two of them were happily at work taking shovelfuls of dirt out of the deepening hole.

When Kate saw the two of them together, she could barely contain herself. "There's something happening between those two, Jamie."

"You're going to get your nose caught if you're not careful, Kate," said her brother.

"What do you mean by that?"

Jamie laughed. "Meg thinks you're too nosy. Now give me a hand here."

The three youngest members of the family worked together. First they skinned all the logs. It was easy to do, but it was dirty work. The poplar trees were so filled with sap and wet with moisture that the logs glistened once the bark was removed. The sap got all over their hands and clothes.

They had to figure out how to attach the long runners to the saddle. Jamie fiddled until he decided to drill a hole in the poles and tie them onto the saddle with cord.

The work on the sled took even longer. They measured the pieces carefully and then cut through the wood with the saw. It was hard-going. The wet logs bound up the saw.

Jamie's arms got tired and his hands blistered. The other kids tried to help, but they were not strong enough. By the time Jamie went to the field to relieve his mother from the plough, they were a long way from finishing.

Slowly but steadily the field was growing. They had ploughed more than an acre now. It did not look like much, but it represented a huge amount of work.

As Jamie walked behind the plough, he admired Baby. The big ox seemed to know exactly what was expected of him and needed very little prodding. He never went very fast but never slowed. He plodded on in a monotonous way, one step after the other, all Jamie had to do was hold the plough in the ground and try to keep the furrows straight. The boy laughed to himself. Baby was the most reliable member of the family, the hardest worker, and maybe the most valuable.

After Jamie had gone to take his turn on the plough, the other two kids wandered out onto the prairie. Robbie looked for birds. He was interested in how they lived, what they ate, and anything and everything about them. For Kate it was exciting just to be out on the prairie and enjoy the expanse of the great sky and the open fields.

They had been out for some time when they heard a movement behind them. They turned to find that Louis had quietly come up behind them on moccasined feet.

"Why do you sneak around so much?" Kate asked.

"When you are on the prairie, you should merge with the land so that the animals do not know you are here," he said in French. "Meg has asked me to call you for lunch."

"We should go."

"It will wait." Louis squatted on his haunches. He was very still and quiet, listening to the sounds around him.

"Do you know about eagles, Louis?" Robbie asked eagerly in English.

"You can often see them soaring high above the prairie. If you watch carefully, you can sometimes see them drop like a stone out of the sky to catch their prey."

"I've seen that."

"The Indians have many stories about eagles. Some even believe they are like gods and their feathers will protect them in battle. There is an eagle's nest high in a big tree down by the river. A few days ago I passed it. The nest was filled with a whole new brood of birds."

Kate found Louis strange and mysterious. Often he was angry and wild, but now he was calm, with a gentle way about him.

"Why do the English settlers fear you so much, Louis?" she asked.

"They know that I tell the truth, and I back down from no man. They know they are wrong to come here to farm without the permission of the Métis people."

He paused for a moment and then spoke slowly and carefully. "The English fear the Métis, just as they fear the Indians, but their need for free land is so strong that their fear will not stop them, just as it did not stop the Bains family. What the Métis fear is that the English will come like a grasshopper plague, and there will be nothing that we can do to stop them."

He got to his feet and looked thoughtfully in every direction across the expanse of prairie like it was an old habit with him. Finally, when he was satisfied, he said, "Come, Meg will have food ready for us," and they returned together to the camp.

The family gathered at the bank of the stream under the big oak tree and sat on the ground eating their meager lunch of cold bannock and thinly sliced salt pork. Louis said nothing while the others bantered in a mixture of English and French.

At the end of the lunch, Peggy gave a brief apology. "I'm sorry, Louis, we don't have much to eat. I have no more to offer."

"You must learn to live off the land like the Métis and Indians," he replied quietly.

"Food is very scarce. Our money is almost gone," she answered.

"Money?" He swept his hand across the landscape. "There is food everywhere in this country. To starve in winter is understandable, but no one should starve now."

"If you can help us, we would be most appreciative."

He nodded, then turned to look at Jamie, Kate, and Robbie. They were playing and chatting, oblivious to the world around them. Louis studied them for a moment and then said only one word in English. "Come."

Jamie looked up in surprise. Louis was already walking away from the camp into the fields toward the west. "What is it?" the boy asked.

"Louis wants all three of you to follow him," his mother replied.

They were confused, but they got to their feet and followed the young Métis. They walked a long way out onto the prairie in single file, Louis in front, then Jamie, Kate, and Robbie dawdling along behind. Louis was attentive to every detail, searching the long grass for movement and signs of life. Finally he held his hand up as a signal and stopped. The others gathered around in a tight circle.

"What did you find?" asked Kate, ever eager.

He looked at her disapprovingly. "The first rule is to be as quiet as possible. If you watch and listen, the prairie comes alive to you. If you talk, or your mind is cluttered with your own thoughts, you will see nothing."

He squatted on his haunches, and all of them sat on the grass around him. He spoke in a clear, precise French so they could understand every word that he had to say

"The Métis people are descended from the French voyageurs, who paddled canoes in the service of the fur trade. They travelled on the rivers from Quebec, on the east coast of this continent, to the Pacific, and from Fort Garry and Hudson Bay to the Arctic Ocean. They married the Cree Indian women, who were born of the lakes and rivers of this land and whose people rode their horses in the buffalo hunts of the prairies. The Métis say their fathers were French and their mothers Cree, and they carry the best of both cultures."

He paused for a moment before continuing. "From our French fathers, the Métis learned about commerce and trading, and from our Cree mothers, we learned how to live on this land. If you listen to what I say, you will learn the ways of survival."

For a full minute or more, he stopped talking as he watched and listened to the sounds around him. Kate, Jamie, and Robbie were completely quiet. When he began again, they hung on every word he said.

"There are many things to learn: when the mushrooms can be collected; where to find deer grazing on the prairie early in the morning; when the fishing in the river is at its best; how to hunt for geese and ducks; when to snare rabbits; and how to catch prairie chickens. If you watch and listen, there are many other things you can learn. As our Cree mothers say, you have to become a part of the land, and it will teach you how to survive."

Louis paused and listened once again before continuing. "Today I will show you how to snare rabbits."

"Do you really catch those nice little rabbits?" asked Kate, full of concern.

"The Indian way is to take only what is needed and to thank the animals for their bounty."

Louis had brought some strong cord. On his belt he carried a knife. It took him only a minute to find some small, strong branches of bushes and fashion them into a snare with the cord that would catch a small animal. They set the snare and moved to another spot that Louis selected.

"If you look closely, you can see a little passageway where rabbits run," he said quietly. "You have to study the grass to find places like that." Jamie made the next snare, following Louis' instructions. Next Kate had a turn, then Robbie.

As they walked back to the camp, Kate and Robbie were excited. They ran ahead to tell Meg about setting the snares while the other two came behind.

"If this family is to survive on the prairie, you will have to become the hunter, Jamie," the young Métis said quietly.

"Will you help me?"

"As best I can, but most will be up to you."

Louis helped Meg dig the hole for the house, and by mid-afternoon they declared that they were finished. The Métis had a cup of tea with them. Then he mounted his horse and rode back to his family's cabin down by the river.

It was close to supper time when Jamie, Kate, and Robbie headed out to check on their snares. Robbie had run a long way ahead. Suddenly he was shouting excitedly, "We've got one! A rabbit! Come and see!" A large, plump grey rabbit was caught in one of their snares. They would eat well that night.

Even though things were so new, the family was developing a routine. Peggy spent most of her time ploughing the field, which slowly grew ever larger. Jamie spelled his mother off as much as possible, but as she became stronger Peggy insisted on doing most of the ploughing herself.

It took two full days for Jamie to finish the sled. He had to carefully cut each log with the saw and then drill holes through them so they could be tied together with strong cord. The trickiest part was attaching the long runners to the sled. The boy fashioned pegs from hardwood so that the runners would swivel and move.

When it was finished, it looked like no masterpiece, but he thought that it might work. They backed the buffalo pony into the long shafts and tied them onto the saddle. Jamie led the horse around the camp to let him get the feel of pulling the sled. The pony adapted very quickly, but the boy wondered how long the sled would take the punishing work that they would give it.

Now that the hole was dug for the house, the next major chore was to build the structure. They needed a log post at each of the four corners of the building and long logs for the sills and roof. The morning after they finished the sled, Jamie and Kate hitched it to the pony, took the axe and headed across the prairie toward the trees that lined the Assiniboine River.

At first Jamie watched the sled carefully. It tailed along behind them beautifully. He smiled to himself. Maybe the sled might work after all.

Once they were into the ride, he began to relax and remembered the lessons that Louis had taught. Be observant; watch for signs of life; become a part of the landscape. He saw the eagles soaring high in lazy circles. Rabbits and gophers fled the hooves of the horse. Jamie made a mental note of where he saw a prairie chicken. One day soon he would come back and get it. As they approached the trees, the sun was high, and it was getting hot. Near the marsh Jamie reined in the horse and rested for a moment. He scanned the horizon and spotted six deer close to the trees a distance away. If he was just able to get one, it would feed the family for a long time.

"Why don't you see if you can find some duck eggs, Kate," he suggested. "I'll go down to cut the logs." She slid off the horse and a moment later disappeared into the long reeds that surrounded the wetlands.

Jamie was gone for two hours, cutting trees and loading them onto the new sled. When he returned for his sister, she not only had six speckled brown eggs, but a duck was neatly tucked in a canvas bag that she carried.

Kate was excited. "I was able to sneak up on the duck while it was sitting on its nest. I caught it in my shawl. But … but now I feel badly." And her face turned into a deep frown.

Jamie smiled at his young sister's plight. "There's lots of ducks in this country, Kate. As Louis said, we have to learn to live off the land. We're going to eat well tonight."

It was Saturday and over a supper of delicious roast duck the family discussed going to the Campbell place. It was Peggy who brought up the issue.

"I've been thinking about tomorrow's meeting," she started.

"I haven't changed my mind," said Meg, decisively. "I couldn't stand them talking about the Dauphin family."

"What if we just listened to what they have to say," Peggy countered.

"But what if I get into an awful fight with them?" Everyone knew that Meg was capable of that.

"You don't have to say anything, Meg. But these people are our neighbours. We can't just ignore them."

Finally Meg relented, but she was not happy about the prospect.

# 7

The next morning was Sunday. Peggy Bains announced to her children that this was their day of rest and no one was going to work. What a relief. Jamie immediately went back to sleep. Kate and Robbie sat in the warmth of the sun and re-read their books for the tenth time. Meg and her mother drank tea and chatted.

By the time the rest of the family stirred into life, the sun was high in the sky. A stiff breeze was rising, and in the west big billowy clouds were developing along the horizon. They had a leisurely breakfast and began to get ready for the party at the Campbell place.

Every member of the family had a few good clothes, but they had been crammed into boxes before they left Ontario. As the clothes came out, one by one, Meg and Peggy tried to shake out the wrinkles while Kate and Robbie hung them from branches of the big oak tree by the stream. Peggy warmed her flatiron by the fire as best she could and tried to get out the creases from the dresses, shirts, and petticoats but with only moderate success.

Every one of them had a good scrubbing in the creek with yellow laundry soap. Then came the long process of dressing. By the time they were ready to go, they all looked more polished than they had for weeks.

Meg wore a long cotton skirt with a top to match that made her look like an attractive young woman. Even her brother Jamie was moved to comment on how pretty she looked. Kate's skirt was an old one that had been bundled up in the bottom of a case. The touching up with the iron had given it new life, but there were still some stubborn wrinkles and creases. The best the two boys could do was to put on a fresh pressed shirt, polish their shoes with some stove black they had brought with them, and slick down their hair with a comb and water from the creek.

Their mother sat by the stream and spent a long time brushing out her long auburn hair. For the first time, she noticed that streaks of grey were beginning to show. She wrapped it up in a tight bun and put on her best dress along with a little sunbonnet that perched neatly on top of her head. Finally, they were all ready to meet the neighbours.

It was four miles to the Campbell place, and the family set out walking a little past noon. The three youngest wanted to ride the buffalo pony, and their mother agreed on condition that everyone got a turn.

Robbie rode the horse first, with Jamie leading with the reins in his hands. The young boy loved being on the pony's back, but he grew impatient because Jamie would not let him ride by himself. He nagged and finally got his way but only on condition that the horse be kept to a walk and no faster.

Robbie managed without any trouble. The high-spirited pony tried to bolt ahead, but the boy held him in check with the reins. It was not long before horse and rider were working together.

They walked at least three miles and were beginning to wonder where the Campbells lived when they spotted the place in among a grove of bushes and trees. It was a wooden house made out of planed boards and painted a fresh white. In front was a dusty road that connected with the trail leading to the Assiniboine River. In behind the house was a small barn and two ploughed fields of about three acres each. There were already two saddled workhorses tied to a rail in front of the house. People were gathering around a long table out in the yard.

The Bains family was warmly welcomed by Mr. Campbell. "Nice to see you, Mrs. Bains ... Peggy. Let me introduce you to the wife. Ruby ... Ruby ... over here. This is Peggy Bains and her family that I was tellin' you about."

Ruby Campbell was a big woman with a happy, rosy face. Her arms were massive, and she seemed to spill out of the new cotton party dress that she wore for the occasion. "So good to meet you, Peggy. Nice to have another woman in the neighbourhood. Too many bachelors in this country if you ask me." She laughed and threw her arm around Peggy's shoulder in a good-natured, friendly way.

"Oh, and who is this pretty young thing?" she continued as she saw Meg. "There's many a young man in these parts that will be happy to see the likes of you, my dear." And she boomed out a laugh again.

Ruby gave a warm welcome to Jamie and Kate and gushed over "young Robbie," as she called him. Then she led the Bains family out into the yard for introductions.

"Now, Meg. You watch out for these two young men, or they'll be at your place faster than a greased pig. You met Albert and this here one is Frank McGill. He has a quarter section west of us."

Frank, like Albert, was a young man in his early twenties, but while Albert was clean-shaven and short, with powerful shoulders, Frank was tall and lanky with a trim mustache and longish hair. Both were wearing their Sunday best with jackets and ties that were too tight and uncomfortable. They had sun-reddened faces, and when they shook Meg's hand, their faces turned an even deeper red.

The guests were sitting on kitchen chairs around a rough pine table that had been set up in the garden beside the house. There was little shade and the sun beat down on them. The wind stirred long grass in the garden and waved the branches of the bushes back and forth restlessly.

Frank tried his best to make conversation about the weather and the planting season while Albert headed off to find chairs. When he did find them, he could not find a piece of level ground to set them on the rough prairie grass.

Once everyone was settled, the two farmers attempted their best to engage Meg in conversation. Kate and Jamie giggled at the sight of these two awkward men competing for their sister's attention.

The Campbells had four children under ten and Robbie wandered off to play with them. The kids did not want to listen to all the boring adult talk.

Jamie and Kate were bored as well and went to look around the farm. The Campbells had taken their homestead three years before and had turned it into a well-established place. In the barn were a dozen chickens along with two pigs. A cow was tethered to a stake out in the meadow and there were sheep, cattle, two horses, and a little colt. Two big garden plots were being readied for planting.

When they came back to the house, Kate found herself drawn into the work by Ruby, who needed an extra hand to help lay out the food that she had prepared. Jamie joined in as well. They were amazed at the food. There was real bread that was puffy and light, just like the bread you could buy in a bakery. Plates of cold sliced pork and boiled eggs were set out on the tables along with potatoes, carrots, and turnips in melted butter.

Ruby saw Jamie eyeing a jug of frothy, cold white milk and poured him a big glass. He gulped it down without taking the glass from his lips. Ruby was the type of woman who knew hungry kids and how to feed them.

Kate took a moment to look around the house. It was like a farmhouse in Ontario. The rooms were spacious, with plaster on the walls, and real windows with drapes that opened and closed. The front room was filled with overstuffed furniture. To Kate it seemed like the Campbells lived in the lap of luxury.

As the spread of food was laid out on the table in the garden, Ruby, Jamie, and Kate joined the others sitting in the yard. They were talking about the Bainses' homesteading plans.

"So what are you going to plant in that field I see you ploughing, Mrs. Bains?" asked Campbell.

"Spring wheat … Red Fife wheat."

The farmer shook his head. "I don't know about that. We only have about ninety days for a crop to ripen in Manitoba before the frost hits us."

"That should be enough time," Peggy replied. "I figure the prairies should be about right for grain crops."

"Risky if you ask me. Cattle. That's what we should be raising out here. Look at all the grazing land and there is more hay than we can ever use."

Albert shook his head sceptically and said, "A woman homesteading. It don't seem right to me. The work is long and hard. Difficult even for a young, strong man. A woman's true role is to help her husband."

Meg had a smirk on her face. "I'm surprised that you think that a woman is important at all on a farm, Albert," she remarked.

"Oh, very important. Looking after the garden and the chickens and the household chores. That's enough for any woman. The rest is man's work."

"That's the natural order of things," agreed Frank.

Now Meg was laughing. "You don't know much about the natural order of things in the Bains family."

Albert leaned forward to emphasize his point and said, "With all due respect, I don't know what that dad blasted government of ours is thinkin' about givin' women the rights to homestead."

"Now there you are talkin' politics all over again," Ruby said, rescuing the discussion by interrupting with her loud voice. "All I can say is anyone with the gumption and get-up-and-go to come out here to the end of civilization and homestead on the prairie should have all the support of everyone in the province. That's what I say."

"Even a woman, Ruby?" asked her husband.

"Well, I don't know about that, but leave all this nonsense alone and come and have a good feed. I bet you young bachelors have not had a woman's cooked meal in all the time that you've been here. Come and get a good tuck-in."

But the really hungry ones were the members of the Bains family. It had been weeks since they had a good filling meal, and all of them went back two or three times to fill up their plates.

This seemed to please Ruby all the more. She kept bringing out platters of food: meats, bread, turnip, carrots, pickles, milk, and more. And that was just the first course. Later she brought out two big pies made with saskatoon berries that they had picked and preserved the year before. Everything was delicious.

Jamie and Kate sat with the others in the garden, their plates on their laps, trying not to spill anything over their clean clothes. The strong May sun made it hot, but the steady prairie breeze cooled their skin. They listened to the conversation, saying nothing.

"Ruby, I was wondering if you had made any plans about school for your children?" Peggy asked.

"There's no schoolin' out in these parts. I've been givin' the readin' and writin' to my own children myself, but the truth is I'm not much of a scholar."

"We need a school."

"The government says we must have fifteen children before they will give us the money for a school. What with my five and your three young ones that makes eight. We need some more homesteaders."

"Our children need an education," replied Peggy. "Aren't there any more children living in the area?"

"Just that big brood of Métis kids livin' down by the river," said Mr. Campbell, "but they're French and Catholic to boot."

This touched a raw nerve in Meg. "What difference does that make?"

"Would you want your brothers and sister goin' to school with them?"

"I don't think that would be a problem, Mr. Campbell, but would the Métis want to go to school with us?" Meg asked, trying to keep her anger in check.

Albert spoke up. "Do you know that Dauphin doesn't even speak English?"

"What's wrong with that?"

"This is a British country."

"There are many people in this country who do not speak English, sir," said Peggy frostily. "They manage to do quite nicely, thank you very much."

"Well, as an Orangeman I'm not in favour of providing education for people like those Dauphins and their brood of children." Albert shot back, appearing very rigid and head-strong. "That young Louis is going around threatening us, including women and children. We don't have to put up with that."

"Things are gettin' out of hand," agreed Campbell.

"The other day he said that this was all Métis land and there should be no English settlers," Albert added, still annoyed. "What are we going to do?"

"The thing that worries me," added Campbell, "is that Louis is the leader of a whole group of young Métis that are living along the river. They've got hunting rifles and horses. They could force us off this land at the point of a gun."

"That's not going to happen to me," declared Frank.

"I'll fight for my land." Albert was getting worked up now. "They're little better than outlaws. I tell you, Campbell, we've got to stop this before it gets out of control."

Jamie was beginning to be alarmed by the tone of the conversation when his mother tried to calm things. "Louis is just a young man."

"Have you sided with the Métis, Mrs. Bains?" Albert demanded.

"We've sided with no one, but let's not lose our heads here."

"Look, Peggy," Campbell said, leaning forward to emphasize his point, "six years ago the Métis rose in rebellion. They took over the whole government of the Red River settlement. Louis Riel was orderin' people around and lockin' good British subjects in the jail. He executed Thomas Scott! Murder is what it was. The Canadian government had to send the army against him. If we aren't careful, these Métis will rise again and who knows what will happen?"

"But I don't see rebellion anywhere," argued Peggy. "I see one young man who makes rash statements. That's not a rebellion."

"That's how it begins. It starts with one man and then it spreads to others and before you know it there is a whole group of malcontents wanting to take our land back. We've got to nip this in the bud. What do the two of you think?" he asked Albert and Frank.

"You're absolutely right," said Albert. "These Métis could be just like the Sioux Indians. Before you know it, we could be attacked and our houses burned. It could be full-scale war. We need to go see this young Louis and let him know in no uncertain terms that there better be no rebellion in these parts or he'll pay a big price."

"I agree with that," concluded Campbell.

"What do you think, Ruby?" asked Peggy. She did not like the way things were developing, and she was hoping Ruby might change the direction of the conversation.

Ruby was very uncomfortable about being put on the spot. "This is politics talk. I —"

Her husband interrupted her and said, "My wife knows nothing about these matters."

Ruby got to her feet and began to clear away the dishes. "It's up to the men."

"Well, I don't think it should be up to men," said Meg, her pretty face showing the tension. "The Métis have had a difficult time. The buffalo have gone. Settlers are moving onto their grazing land. What would you do if your way of life was threatened?"

Peggy was concerned about the hardened opinions of the men. They were not going to listen to arguments and change their minds. But at that moment she was particularly concerned about her daughter. Meg had a hot temper and would not back down from anyone. They would have to live with their neighbours for a long time.

"We've had enough of this talk," said Campbell, with a tone of irritation. "I'm not sayin' that these people are going to mount another rebellion, Mrs. Bains. I don't know about that. But this young Louis has to be brought under control. He can't go around telling people they have no right to their homesteads. And I say that we should go down and tell him to stop right now. What do the rest of you think?"

"I'm with you, Campbell," agreed Albert immediately. His face had taken on a tight angry look that was a mixture of hostility and frustration.

"Cease and desist. That's what we tell him," added Frank. "Let's pay him a visit." He was not as militant as Albert, but he seemed to follow his lead.

Meg was about to challenge them when her mother's hand locked on her forearm and brought her to a stop. The unspoken but firm message was that she was to say nothing more. Peggy answered them with a very clear message. "I don't like this one bit. It seems to me you're seeking out trouble."

"You have to be firm with these people, Peggy," said Campbell. "You haven't lived in these parts long enough to understand. These Métis will push us around until we stand up to them."

Peggy leaned forward to make her point. "These people, as you call them, Mr. Campbell, have lived in this area for a long time."

"These people are Métis … half Indian, half French Canadian," replied Albert sharply. "They don't deserve our respect."

Peggy got to her feet, and the other members of her family followed. There was nothing more to be said. She knew people with fixed opinions could not be reasoned with.

Kate and Jamie had listened to the whole exchange. As they moved out of earshot from the others, Kate whispered to her brother. "We should have told them that Louis taught us all sorts of things. That might change their minds about him."

"They don't want to listen, Kate," her brother replied.

Peggy and Meg helped Ruby bring the dishes into the house while the men sat in the yard talking. "That certainly was a beautiful spread, Ruby," Peggy said, trying to keep up a pleasant appearance. "I hope my children didn't eat you out of house and home. It's been a while since we have had good cooking like this."

"Any time you want to send your young ones over here we'll just feed them up, Peggy," Ruby offered, laughing in her big-hearted way. "As you can see, I'm an ample woman and I do like to see people eat."

As they finished with the kitchen chores, the men were preparing to leave on their horses. The three of them looked deadly serious. Albert had a rifle in a long holster on his saddle and Campbell brought a shotgun out of the house. The men were ready for anything. Peggy watched for the opportunity and then called Jamie and Kate aside. Meg listened.

"Did you hear what they were saying?" Peggy whispered.

"Are they going to do something to the Dauphins?" Kate asked.

"Louis needs to be warned that they are coming. They've got guns. Who knows what could happen? Do you know where the Dauphins live, Jamie?" said their mother.

"We've seen their house down by the river."

"Listen carefully. I want the two of you to take the buffalo pony and ride out of here like you are going back to the homestead. If the men ask where you're going, tell them that you have to do some chores. When you're out of sight, head down to the Dauphin place as fast as the pony will take you. Warn them that Campbell and the others are coming and that they are carrying weapons."

Both Kate and Jamie nodded and said, "We're on our way."

# 8

As they rode out onto the prairie, Kate and Jamie noticed a storm was beginning to gather in the west. Big thunderclouds rose high into the sky. The wind had picked up and was blowing the long prairie grass like waves at sea.

At first they rode the buffalo pony in an easy loping run, but once they were a distance away from the Campbell place, Jamie urged the horse into a gallop. As they left, the two bachelors were still getting ready to ride down to the Dauphin place. The buffalo pony was faster, and they were a long way ahead, but they did not have much of a lead.

They rode without speaking in the direction of their camp until Jamie turned to his sister. "Can you still see them, Kate?"

She turned around. "They're just leaving the Campbell place."

"Maybe we don't have enough time to get to the Dauphins' and back."

The bald prairie gave them no cover. They rode in the direction of their homestead so that if they were seen it would appear that they were going back to their camp. It was essential that Campbell and the farmers not know where they were heading.

For a long distance, the buffalo pony galloped hard but then began to tire. He slowed to a steady run and despite urging would not go any faster.

They were almost at the camp when Kate said that the farmers and their big horses were out of sight. Still Jamie was cautious. He waited until they were in among some brush and then changed direction and headed toward the Assiniboine River. A few minutes later, they were passing the marsh and entered into the trees.

At first Jamie could not find a trail. They had to push through underbrush and dodge around trees. They slowed to a walk, and the boy was considering getting off the buffalo pony to lead him through this maze when they came across a rough cart road.

They went down a steep hill and found themselves at the river's edge. On the other side, they could see fields and farms. It was not long before they broke out of the trees and came into a clearing.

Two horses and a cow were grazing in a small pasture. A second field was a huge vegetable garden, ploughed and ready for planting. There was a stable for the animals and in the middle of the clearing was a log house with smoke rising from the chimney.

"That's Louis' horse," said Kate, pointing to the bay pony in the pasture. "This must be the Dauphin place."

"Monsieur Dauphin … Monsieur Dauphin!" Jamie called as they rode across the field to the house.

The door opened and four young children came spilling outside to see who was calling their name in this isolated place. Louis appeared, followed by a young girl about Jamie's age. Dauphin filled the doorway beside a woman with long black hair who appeared to be his wife.

"Comment ça va, Jamie, Kat'leen?" asked Dauphin. "What brings you here?"

"It's the farmers, sir," began Kate breathlessly in French. "They're coming on their big horses to see you and Louis and …"

The pony danced around in a spirited way. Wet lather from the long hard run had gathered on his neck and along his flanks. Louis took hold of his halter and the horse quieted.

"Calm yourself, *mes amis*. Come inside and rest." The Métis came to stand beside them.

"We can't Monsieur Dauphin," replied Jamie. "We came to warn you that Mr. Campbell and two other farmers are on their way here."

"What for?"

"They say they want to talk to Louis …"

"They're angry," added Kate excitedly.

Louis had said nothing. Dauphin remained calm. "But why do they want to talk to Louis?"

Jamie tried to explain as best he could, but his French was not up to it. "They say he's going around threatening people, telling them that it's … it's not right for English people to be coming here. They're afraid of rebellion."

Kate's French was better. "We were off at the Campbell place, and they were saying all these awful things about Louis and … and the Métis. We told them it wasn't true, but they wouldn't listen. They're coming here. Three men: Mr. Campbell and two other young farmers."

Louis let the halter go and stepped back. His lean dark face had taken on an angry look. "Do they come with weapons?" he asked in French.

"You mean with guns and things?" asked Kate.

"Yes. They have rifles and shotguns," answered Jamie.

"They'll not take me that easily!" Louis was angry now, furious. "English fools. I'll show them."

Jamie was panicked. "They say that they are just coming down to warn you."

"They're not going to tell me what to do," he exclaimed in French. "This is Métis country! Métis land!"

"Louis! Control yourself!" his father commanded.

"Control myself! What for?" He was shouting now.

"You will get into trouble if you act foolishly!"

Louis turned on his father angrily and said, "Control myself. That's what you always say. We wait, and we do nothing and now we are losing our land. What will be left for the Métis people? I ask you Father! What is left? There are no more buffalo. Soon our pasture land will be gone. There will be nothing for the Métis, nothing!"

He pushed his way through the children, entered the cabin, and a moment later emerged carrying a rifle. He strode across the yard toward his horse.

"Louis, where are you going?" his father called after him. "Louis …" But his son did not answer.

The young Métis got his horse from the corral. He thrust the long rifle into a holster on the saddle and mounted. As he rode out of the yard, his father tried one last time. "Louis, I want to know where you are going!"

"I am not going to sit here and wait for the English to tell me what to do!" he shouted in reply. Then he kicked the sides of his horse and rode away from the others.

"*Mon Dieu,*" muttered his father to himself. "I can feel the trouble brewing."

"Maybe we shouldn't have brought you the news," said Jamie awkwardly.

Dauphin looked up at Kate and Jamie mounted on the back of their horse. His face reflected sadness. "What can I say to him?" he asked. "After the rebellion the future of the Métis looked bright, but now the clouds are gathering again. Louis wants me to try and stop the settlers, but they come here in thousands. Soon it will be hundreds of thousands. How can we stop them? What should the Métis people do?"

He hung his head for a moment and then looked up. "Louis is … you have a word for it in English. *Oui, un* hothead," and he laughed. "That's a good word for it. A hothead. I fear what will happen when he meets up with Campbell and the others."

The mention of Campbell's name brought Jamie back to reality. "We have to go, Monsieur Dauphin," he said. The boy turned and looked back at the trail they had come on, half expecting to see the farmers emerging from the trees. "They'll be here soon, and we don't want them to know that we warned you."

"*Oui*, I understand. You will find a trail up to the pasture lands on the other side of the field, there," and he pointed in the direction Louis had disappeared. "It's not far back to your place. Go and we'll speak later about this."

Jamie kicked the buffalo pony, and they rode across the field to the trees. It took only a moment to find the trail. He turned the horse uphill and began the long climb up to the prairies.

As they broke out of the trees onto the open range, they could see the change in the weather. The sky had darkened, and in the west big thunderclouds towered thousands of feet into the sky. The wind stirred the aspen trees, flashing the white undersides of the leaves.

"We have to get things at the camp under cover before the storm hits," Jamie shouted. Their buffalo pony responded, and they rode the distance in a loping run.

The pony would need a good rubdown, but that would have to wait. Kate tied him up to a wheel of the cart, and the two of them dashed about the camp putting things under the canvas lean-to or storing them under the shelter of the cart.

They had almost forgotten about Campbell and the two bachelor farmers until they saw the three big workhorses ride into their camp.

"Wise to get things under cover," said Campbell in his easy drawl. "A prairie storm can turn into a deluge."

Jamie and Kate dropped what they were doing and walked toward the horses. Campbell was in his farmer clothes, but Albert and Frank were still wearing their Sunday best.

"Jamie, we were wonderin' if you'd come down to the Dauphin place with us?" Campbell continued. "Before we left your mother told us that you speak a good French. Old Dauphin, there, don't speak a word of the Queen's language."

The boy was not expecting this. "Well ... I —"

"This is your fight, same as ours, boy," added Albert abruptly. "Young Louis made threats against your family."

Jamie glanced at his sister. Kate looked as perplexed as he felt. If they rode with Campbell, it would look like they had sided against the Dauphins, but how could they refuse?

"There's a storm coming, and we're not ready and —"

"Come on, boy," Campbell said. "Your horse is already saddled up. It's not far. You'll be back here before the storm breaks. This is just a little social call."

What could he do? And what would the Dauphins think if he arrived with the farmers?

"All right," Jamie said finally. "But only if Kate comes along. Her French is better than mine."

"Come on then. Let's ride."

# 9

"Why did you agree?" Kate whispered to her brother as they went to get their horse.

"We're going to translate. Nothing else."

"But Jamie ..."

"Shush ... They'll hear us."

They climbed up on the buffalo pony and began to head toward the river. The workhorses set a slow lumbering gait, and the pony matched their pace. The men were talking to each other. Kate and Jamie listened without comment.

"I tell you the Métis don't know how to use this land," said Albert. "Look at it. Still rough prairie. They use it for grazin' and nothin' else. The most they do is take off a little hay."

Campbell agreed. "They've never put a plough to it, and they never will. They're hunters. That's all. They do a little gardening, grow a few vegetables, but you'll never see them out here workin' the land."

"Life is one big long party for them," added Frank.

Campbell nodded. "That's true. A Métis wedding will go on for days. They dance until they drop."

"Have you ever gone to one of their weddings, Campbell?"

"Can't say as I have, but I've heard all about it. They'll sing songs and dance in their moccasins to fiddle music. It's no wonder that this country is so backward."

"That's why we have to sort this thing out right now," said Albert, the most strident of the group. "Every one of us has been put on the good green earth to work. Not party all the time."

Jamie wanted to say something, but he felt he could not challenge these adults. The storm was gathering strength. The wind was beginning to lash the long grass back and forth. The sky was darkening as the thunderclouds swept overhead. But the rain held off.

They entered the trees and went down the slope until they found the cart trail. Kate and Jamie led the others along the trail until they could hear the rush of the river as it flowed across stones. A little farther on, they came into the clearing. Beyond they could see other Métis farms along the river stretching into the distance.

Monsieur Dauphin was out in the garden with his wife. The young children were playing. Louis was nowhere in sight. They rode up to the stable and dismounted. Dauphin came and joined them while the other members of the family lingered close by.

*"Bonjour,"* Dauphin greeted them. *"Comment ça va, Monsieur Campbell?"* The Métis nodded politely to the others.

"What's he saying?" asked Frank nervously.

"He just said hello," explained Kate.

"Where's Louis?" demanded Albert sharply.

Kate translated and Dauphin replied in French. "He says he's not here," she said, translating back into English.

"When will he be back?"

Again Kate translated and again Dauphin replied. "He doesn't know."

"Tell him that we have to see Louis now. It's important."

After the translation, Kate explained. "He has no idea where Louis is or when he will be back."

This only served to upset Albert even more. "Well, that's not good enough. We've come to give him a message."

"But Dauphin explained that he's not here," Kate said, getting annoyed.

"I think he's lying!" Albert's jaw stuck out in a determined way as if he intended to show how stern he was.

Kate immediately translated this into French. "Albert says that he thinks you are lying."

"Lying!" Dauphin became furious. "I am known as a man of my word. Ask any of the Métis people, and they will say the same!"

"What did he say?" demanded Albert.

"He's angry because you called him a liar," explained Kate.

"Why'd you translate that?" Albert was shocked.

"Because you wanted me to translate!" she replied hotly. Kate was not going to take abuse from anyone.

"Let me translate, Kate," interrupted Jamie. Things were getting out of hand, and he had to try to calm them down.

"I tell you, these people should be made to speak English," said Frank with a disgusted tone.

Jamie was reluctant to translate this into French, but Dauphin demanded to know what had been said. Hesitantly the boy explained.

This put Dauphin in a fury. "French has always been the language of the Métis people — French and Cree. We have lived here for decades. You are the newcomers. You should learn to speak French rather than us learning English!"

Jamie tried to think of a way to defuse the tension, but it was too late. Things had gone from bad to worse.

Now Campbell joined the argument. "Dauphin, we came here to tell you that your son cannot go around telling people to get off their own land. These people have been granted homesteads for these lands by the government. Louis has no right to tell them to get out! We want it stopped, and we want it stopped now!"

Dauphin turned coldly serious. "You leave my son alone. He has done no one any harm."

"He can't go around threatening people. It's wrong!"

"You heard me. Leave him alone or you will have to deal with me!" Dauphin was angry now.

Jamie was getting breathless with the translating, but despite his limited French, he was doing it so well that the two men were talking directly to each other. He was just the instrument of their communication.

"And I'm telling you we've had enough of this threatening business!"

"You've said too much already, Campbell. Now, you are standing on my land, and I want you to get off it right now."

When Jamie translated this last comment, it put Albert into a rage. "No self-respecting Orangeman should have to put up with this sort of behaviour from the likes of a Métis."

"Leave!" demanded Dauphin again.

"Nobody is going to tell us to leave!"

"What do you want to do?" asked Frank. Even he was starting to get upset.

"Maybe we should give him a taste of our type of medicine," Albert replied in a rage. "If he wants trouble, then we'll bring it to him." He went to his horse and pulled his rifle out of its long holster.

"Let's calm down, boys," said Campbell. He was getting alarmed.

"He's ordering us off this land," Albert shot back. "We're not going to put up with that!"

It was just as well that the conversation was going too fast for Jamie to translate.

"You come and insult me," Dauphin continued in French. "Insult the Métis people. I want you to leave now!"

"Look!" Campbell pointed across the field to the fence in the distance. Louis was standing in front of the split-rail fence with his rifle folded across his arms. Crouched behind the fence, four young Métis men were spaced twenty feet apart. Each of them held a repeater rifle, and they were pointing them right at the English settlers.

"My God!" said Frank, in panic. "We could never get out of here alive."

Louis walked toward them across the field, a calm, determined expression on his face.

"Let's leave now!" Frank had lost his nerve, but the others were rooted to the spot. It was too late to flee.

When Louis reached them, he looked back to check to see if the others were ranged along the fence. "What is happening, Father?" he asked calmly in French. Then he repeated it in English. "What's happening here?"

The farmers were too alarmed and disorganized to speak. Jamie answered for them all. "They came to talk to you, Louis."

"Then why do you bother my father with loud, angry words?" He was continuing to speak in English with a heavy accent.

Campbell tried to explain. "It's just … we wanted to get a message to you and …"

"If it's me you want to speak to, then say it to my face."

"It's just that —"

"Why do you have guns?" Albert broke in angrily. "You've got your friends out there. Is this an uprising?"

"You've got guns, too."

"We need them for our protection."

"That's why we have ours, as well."

It was silent for a moment, a standoff. The farmers had arrived full of indignation and bluster. The arrival of Louis and his friends had taken the wind out of their sails.

"What did you come to tell me?" Louis asked again.

Campbell was nervous, but he tried to explain. "We came to talk to you about the threats you have made to English settlers."

"I make no threats."

"You've told people that this is Métis land, and they should leave."

"Yes, I have said that, and I have said that we have hay privileges on this land. That is true, but I have threatened no one."

"You threatened Peggy Bains. She told us."

"I did not threaten her. I told her this was Métis land. That was all." Louis pointed at Jamie. "He was there. Tell him what I said."

Jamie glanced at his sister. Events were happening too fast to control. The situation was explosive. "You ... you just told us that it was Métis land."

"And what else, Jamie?" Campbell demanded.

"That's all."

"No it's not. What else did he say?"

The boy felt the pressure. He had to tell the truth. Jamie looked at the three farmers and then back at the young Métis. "Louis said that the homesteading papers that we got from the government were ... were worthless."

"You see," said Campbell triumphantly.

"But he didn't threaten us," Jamie continued. "All he said was that our papers were useless, and we should get off the land."

"That's the same as threatenin'. You were intimidatin' people, Louis. Telling untruths! Admit it!"

"I will not admit to a thing I have not done."

"You were threatenin' people — women and children!" Albert shouted.

"Now you are threatening me?" Louis' anger was beginning to build.

"I'm just tellin' you that we're not goin' to put up with you goin' around threatenin' people."

"I threaten no one!" Louis was shouting now.

"You heard what the boy said!" Albert was pointing his finger.

"He didn't threaten us," Jamie repeated, but they were not listening to him.

"Get off of our land!" Louis shouted. "And you, too, Jamie Bains. Get off our land and don't come back!"

"Really, Louis, I didn't say you threatened us. I … I was just telling the truth," Jamie tried to explain.

"Quiet, boy!" Albert ordered.

"He didn't threaten anyone." Jamie was pleading to be heard.

"Be quiet, boy," shouted Albert with a bitter edge to his voice. His powerful shoulders were tensed as if he was expecting an attack. "He is just tryin' to twist things." Then he turned back to Louis. "You were out there threatenin' people, and we won't have it! Understand!" he yelled. "We don't care if you've got all the Métis behind you. You're not going to go around threatenin' settlers."

Louis backed up a step. He shifted the long rifle in his arms. Then he spoke with a low ominous edge to his voice. "I want you to get out of here. All of you. Get out of here before something happens that you don't like!"

"See! Threats again!" Albert countered triumphantly.

Kate was shocked at the turn of events. "We weren't part of this, Louis. Really we weren't."

"Get out of here. Leave. I want nothing more to do with you English. Every last one of you are nothing but trouble. Especially members of the Bains family!" He looked right at Jamie. "You play at being friends with us, and all the time you plot to destroy the Métis people."

Jamie had a horrible sinking feeling in his chest. What had he done? He swung into the saddle and Kate climbed up behind him. The Dauphin family stood on the ground watching them with sullen, angry eyes. They were looking at Jamie as if he had betrayed them to the enemy.

As the four horses rode away from the Métis farm, the rain started to fall.

# 10

As they rode up the cart road, the rain turned into a deluge. Lightning flashed across the sky, and thunder rumbled and rolled through the valley. The rain pelted down, soaking through Jamie's jacket and saturating Kate's sweater, blouse, and skirt.

The buffalo pony was dripping wet. He splashed through instant puddles on the cart road. Jamie spurred him on, anxious to get as far away from the three farmers as possible.

It was already growing dark, and the thunderstorm darkened the bush even more, making it increasingly difficult to see the way ahead. Jamie found the spot they had come down the hill, turned off the trail, and began heading up the steep incline. The others were a long way behind and would never find them among the trees and heavy undergrowth.

The boy was in turmoil. Why did he have to open his mouth and give them the chance to say that Louis had threatened the family? Why did he agree to go along with them to translate? He should have known that the men would distort everything in order to make Louis look like a criminal.

Their horse strained to climb the hill. His iron-shod hooves slipped on the mud. Jamie leaned forward and clutched onto the horse's side with his knees to hold himself in the saddle. Kate gripped him tightly around the waist. Neither of them spoke, but both felt overwhelmed by the feeling that they had betrayed their friends. Didn't the Dauphins give them the pony they were riding on? Didn't Louis show them how they could hunt to survive in this country?

As they came to the crest of the hill and broke through the trees they saw the prairie awash in sheets of rain pouring from a black and turbulent sky. Lightning flashed. Thunder rumbled. For an instant their pony shied, but Jamie quickly brought him under control.

Kate was trembling from the cold and the wet clothes that clung to her body. Another streak of lightning flashed, and sudden terror shook through her. This was a wild and uncontrolled place. They could wander for days out on this prairie and never find a sign of life.

"What about Mother, Meg, and Robbie?" Kate shouted into Jamie's ear.

The thought transfixed the boy. Were they still out on the prairie trail, walking back from the Campbell place? He cursed himself. Why had they gone with Campbell and the others? The storm had been coming all day. They had abandoned the family without shelter on the prairie.

Jamie urged the horse into a gallop. They raced through the rain-soaked prairie lands as fast as their fleet pony could take them. Water sprayed from the horse's hooves; the wind buffeted them; they plunged through big puddles and thick prairie grass, galloping on without pause until they came into sight of the campsite.

"Mother! Meg!" Jamie shouted as their horse plunged into the camp.

"Mummy, are you there?" Kate hollered.

"Here, Jamie! Kate! We're under the lean-to."

Kate leaped off the horse and ran to her mother under the shelter. She was trembling from a combination of cold and fear and overwhelming relief to find her family safe under the canvas lean-to.

"You're soaked, Katie. There now. Don't be frightened. You're going to be fine," Peggy said, soothing her youngest daughter.

The wind and rain lashed at Jamie's face. He pulled the saddle from the pony, quickly tied a hobble around his two front legs, and set him loose.

He got down on his hands and knees and crawled under the lean-to with the other members of the family to get what shelter it offered. It did not do much. Gusts of wind blew spray in upon them, and water flowed in from all sides, but at least it provided some protection from the deluge.

Peggy had covered Kate with a blanket and was helping her take off her clothes and put on something warm and dry. The young girl found it such a relief to listen to her mother's soothing voice.

"We got back to camp just before the storm," Peggy explained. "It's been coming down in torrents ever since. But where have the two of you been?"

Jamie was ashamed to explain but knew he must. First he struggled to take off his wet clothes, dried himself as best he could, and put on the only dry shirt and pants that he owned. Then the five members of the Bains family huddled together under the canvas sheet, trying to stay warm and dry. Soon the wind began to drop, and the rain turned into a heavy, steady drizzle.

Slowly Jamie explained how they had gone to the Dauphin place with the farmers. "It was just one long argument from beginning to end." The boy stopped and listened to the rain hitting the canvas sheet just above his head. There was no easy way to tell this. "And then Louis showed up with four of his friends, and they were all carrying rifles."

"The Métis had rifles?" asked Peggy. She was alarmed.

"Albert and Campbell had weapons, as well," explained Jamie. "It was so dangerous. Anything could have happened. Then a big argument started. Mr. Campbell said that Louis threatened our family. I told them it wasn't true, but no one would listen."

"They wouldn't listen to anyone," agreed Kate. "The farmers just wanted to blame Louis and say that he threatened people."

"It sounds to me like they were the ones threatening," said their mother.

Jamie continued the story. "I told them that Louis had said the homestead papers we got were worthless, and they said that was evidence he was threatening us. I told them that wasn't true. I pleaded with them, but they wouldn't listen. Then even Louis got mad at me."

"Louis got mad at you?" Meg asked.

"He thought I was blaming him, and he ordered us off their property and ..." The boy paused for a moment, trying to search for the right words to explain what happened. "It just went from bad to worse. Louis was shouting, and then Mr. Campbell and Albert were shouting. No one was listening."

"He wants nothing more to do with the English," Kate concluded. "Louis said we were nothing but trouble, especially the Bains family."

"What do you mean?" Meg was alarmed.

"He ordered us to leave," Jamie tried to explain.

"What have you done, Jamie!" Meg was beside herself.

"He wouldn't listen!"

"But you shouldn't have taken the side of the farmers against the Métis!"

"We didn't, Meg!" Jamie pleaded with her to understand.

His sister was devastated. "What am I going to do, Mother?"

"Now, now. It can't be that bad." Peggy tried to console her daughter.

"What if I never see him again!"

"Don't worry, he's bound to understand once he thinks things over."

Jamie felt terrible. He had betrayed his sister. Meg had always supported him and helped him and now he paid her back like this. What could he do to make things right?

The Bains family grew quiet as they listened to the dreary sound of the rain drumming on the canvas. A puddle of water was growing at one end of the shelter. Overhead, in the old oak tree, an owl hooted into the wet night. Slowly, one by one, they went to sleep.

The rain continued for an hour or more and then gradually slowed and stopped. But water was everywhere. In the middle of the night, the puddles swelled. The blankets soaked through, and in the morning they woke up to find themselves lying in water.

Robbie jumped up with a start. "I'm all wet," he said, pulling one of the blankets with him.

"Robbie, don't do that," Kate said, clutching other blankets around her, trying to keep warm, but a moment later she felt the water creep up her back and leapt up. "I'm soaked!"

The two youngest Bains children stood just outside the lean-to in their water-drenched clothes. "Oh, Mother. Why did we have to come to this place?" asked Kate despondently.

The long prairie grass drooped into the mud, and the stream surged along with new energy. But as they stood there, the sun rose over the horizon into a clear, cloudless sky. Rays glinted off a thousand water drops, and the warmth spread across the land giving it new life and vitality.

Kate stepped back so that she felt the full rays on her face. She slipped off the blanket that she was clutching over her shoulders. The wet clothes clung to her body, but it did not matter. She felt luxuriously warm in the early summer sun.

The others got up and soon they were spreading all of their belongings out on the grass to dry. Peggy inspected the food and found that the flour and oatmeal were still dry thanks to the tin boxes they were stored in.

Jamie struggled to get a fire going so they could have a breakfast of porridge but finally gave up. They would have to wait to eat until things dried out.

Meg was moping around the campsite. Jamie went up to her cautiously. "I'll make it up to you, Meg. Really I will," he promised, but she barely acknowledged him.

After they spread out their blankets and wet clothes to dry, their mother went off with Jamie to hitch up Baby, the ox. They wrestled the plough into position and prodded the big animal. The plough slid easily into the ground.

"The rainfall has made the ground softer," she said as she held the handles of the plough. "It's pulling through the ground much easier than before."

Jamie went back to the place where they were building the house and found his two sisters staring into the hole. When he joined them, he saw what they were looking at. About a foot of water lay in the bottom.

"We'll have to wait until it drains away," said Meg. "But we can put in the four corner-posts."

Jamie had cut and hauled the posts a couple of days before. Robbie was recruited to help, and the four of them rolled the posts to each corner. By the time they got the posts standing, and packed firmly in place, they were wet and covered in mud. As they finished, they stood back to look at the four upright posts, the first structure to break the prairie landscape from the Métis settlement to the Campbell place.

Jamie was haunted by the image of Louis condemning him and the entire Bains family. "Meg, maybe I should go down to talk to Louis," he suggested after getting the posts in place.

"No."

"But I could explain to him that I never accused him of threatening our family."

"You'll just confuse things all the more, Jamie."

"But Meg!"

"I said no! I don't want you going anywhere close to him." She was very upset.

What more could he do? Now Meg didn't even trust him to offer a simple explanation. He felt completely useless.

The boy went to catch the buffalo pony and hitched him to the sled. The four Bains children went across to the field their mother was ploughing and found her covered in mud from her feet to her head but more enthusiastic than ever.

"This rain was a godsend. I'm able to plough twice as much as before. We're going to make a success of this farm. I can feel it," she said with a broad smile on her face.

"We're here to load some sod for the walls of the house," Meg explained. "We thought it would be easier to take some of the sod that you ploughed up."

They began the tedious job of pulling off the sod and wrestling it onto the sled. Often they had to cut part of it with the shovel. The sod was easier to handle now that it was softened with the rain, but it was heavy, dirty work. Their hands and feet got caked with mud, and their clothes became filthy.

Once they got a load onto the sled, Jamie led the buffalo pony over to the house. He had been worried that the sled would pull apart with the heavy load, but it worked very well. Even fully loaded, the horse could skid it over the grass easily. At the house site they unloaded the sod, one piece at a time, and stacked the pieces like bricks to build the wall. They started on the north wall, and by lunch time it was already a foot high.

Meg had been very quiet most of the morning, and over lunch she sat by herself, looking across the prairie as if half expecting Louis to ride up as if nothing had happened, but he did not come. There was not a sign of life anywhere on the prairie.

"What are we going to do about Meg and Louis?" Jamie whispered to Kate.

"I don't know."

"Maybe I should go to the Dauphin place."

"She'd never forgive you."

"What if she didn't know about it? Would you help me?"

"When do you want to try?"

"Soon."

Meg glanced up at them suspiciously, and they had to abandon their secret conversation. The rest of the afternoon Jamie searched for a chance to talk privately with Kate, but the opportunity never came.

In the afternoon Jamie took a turn on the plough while the others continued the steady work of filling the sled with sod and building the walls of the house. As evening gathered, Peggy came to tell Jamie to quit work for the day and helped him remove the yoke from Baby.

When they were finished, the two of them stood looking at the black furrows. They had five acres of ploughed land now, and though it was still a small field, to the two of them who had put in the hours of work and sweat to create it, the field appeared vast.

Peggy put her arm around her son's shoulders. "Can you imagine what it will look like in three months time?" she said with a dreamy expression in her eyes. "Golden Red Fife wheat swaying in the breeze, heavy with ripe kernels, just waiting for the harvest."

She was absolutely focused on her dream of creating the farm, and nothing, not the Campbells, not the Dauphins, would distract her. The family's future depended on the wheat crop, and she was determined to make it a success.

That night the swarms of black flies and mosquitoes re-turned with a vengeance. They kept smudge pots of smoul-dering grass burning all night, but by morning they had been bitten on the face, and any other spot of exposed skin. At least when the sun came up the insects fled, and they had some relief.

The first thing in the morning Jamie announced that he was going to go down to the river to cut logs to support the roof of the house. Casually he said that he thought Kate should come along with him to help. The boy waited for a reaction, knowing that would be their one chance to escape, but no one suspected a thing.

Jamie and Kate hitched the sled to the buffalo pony, climbed on his back, and set off across the prairie in an easy gait. As they rode, they set in place their detailed plan to contact the Dauphin family.

Once they got to the edge of the trees, they unhitched the sled and went to cut the logs. Jamie selected the trees, cut them down, and trimmed off the branches. Kate tied one end of a rope onto the logs and the other onto the horse's saddle. Then she guided the pony to the top of the hill as he pulled the log behind him. Once all the logs were at the top, it took both of them to load them onto the sled and tie them down.

When they were finished, they were ready to carry out their plan. It was still mid-morning. They would not be missed back at camp for hours.

"Let's go, Kate," Jamie said, swinging into the saddle. His sister climbed up behind him. Leaving the sled behind, the horse and riders plunged through the trees and down the hill to the cart road. Jamie urged the pony into a run and within minutes they were at the edge of the clearing.

They stopped for a moment to take stock of the scene. Dauphin, his wife, and two of the children were working in the garden. Younger children were playing near the house.

Louis was nowhere to be seen. They rode over to a fence near the garden, dismounted, tied the pony to the fence, and walked across the field to meet them.

*"Bonjour, Madame Dauphin, Monsieur, comment ça va?"*

*"Ça va bien,"* said Dauphin. He leaned on his hoe and regarded them suspiciously.

Jamie started to speak in his halting French. "I … I felt I needed to explain about Campbell and … and the others."

Dauphin grunted and said nothing. "We came with them because they asked us to translate. We … we didn't know what they were going to do."

"That's true, Monsieur Dauphin," added Kate. "They put words into Jamie's mouth."

"Louis never threatened us," continued Jamie. "He was upset, yes, and angry at us. You know what he is like, but he never threatened us."

"And Jamie explained that, Monsieur Dauphin, you remember," continued Kate, "but they wouldn't listen. They just went on and on and …"

The Métis man was nodding, but still he said nothing. Jamie picked up where Kate left off. "Mr. Campbell and the others wanted to accuse Louis of something terrible, or they wanted him to do something foolish, I don't know, but we weren't part of it. You have to believe us."

Dauphin looked at them for a long time before replying. *"Oui,* I believe you. But that encounter taught me a lesson." He spoke slowly and deliberately, considering every word carefully. "There is a rift between the Métis and the English, and some people are working to make that rift even wider so that one day there will be no talking between the two groups. Even no talking between friends."

Kate quickly saw the point. "We can't let that happen between us, Monsieur Dauphin."

"You are right, *ma fille*, but it will be difficult. You will see. It will become more difficult as time goes on."

"We have to get back home," said Jamie. "We just wanted you to know that you are welcome at our place anytime. You and Louis and any member of your family."

"*Merci*, Jamie. You are most generous."

The boy smiled and replied, "We will never match the generosity of the Dauphins."

As Kate and Jamie walked back toward the pony, Dauphin called out to them. "When you come all this way to see a Métis you don't go home empty-handed." When they looked back, they saw the happy, generous man whom they had first met.

Dauphin strode across the garden calling to one of his boys about Kate's age. There was much commotion as the Dauphin kids attacked the henhouse and emerged with a dozen brown and white eggs. When Kate and Jamie rode out of the clearing, their pockets were filled.

"How are we going to explain this to mother?" Jamie asked, laughing.

"I guess we are just going to have to say that the ducks have grown a lot bigger," Kate replied with her characteristic giggle.

They need not have worried. Ducks, geese, or hens, it made no difference. These were eggs, and to the hungry members of the Bains family they would be simply delicious. When they got back home, the family stopped work, and Peggy cooked up a big feed of scrambled eggs. No one questioned where they had come from.

They paused only long enough to eat, and then it was back to work. The jobs were unending: ploughing, building the house, cleaning the camp, cooking, washing dishes, washing clothes, setting out the snares. There was so much to do and so little time to do it.

Meg had been quiet all day and that evening she went for a long walk to be alone. No more had been said about Louis, but everyone knew that Meg was pining for the young Métis.

The next morning the four Bains children were trying to figure out how to attach the beams for the roof without nails when they heard the stomp of a horse's hoof behind them. Turning, they saw Louis Dauphin was sitting on his bay pony watching them.

In that moment, Meg's mood was completely transformed. She laughed, trying to cover up her excitement, then turned away in a sudden moment of shyness. She was annoyed that he had stayed away and overwhelmingly happy that he had finally returned.

Louis tried to act as if he had never been absent. "It looks like you're having some trouble," he said in English. "Do you need a hand?" He swung out of the saddle and joined in with the work, but he, too, had a shy smile on his face and stole quick glances at Meg.

By noon they had the main beams for the roof tied in place with rope. Over lunch Louis questioned where they planned to place the front entrance to the house. "On the prairie, doors and windows should always face south," he explained in French. "In winter it is the wind you need protection from. Storms sweep in from the west and the north, but the coldest winds are from the east. If your house looks south, facing the sun, with its back to the wind, you'll remain cosy and warm."

The original plan was to put the door in the east side of the house, and once Louis convinced them to change, they had to cut a new door and block up the other with sod. By mid-afternoon they had finished. Louis said that he had some chores to do and rode off to his home.

After a supper of wild rabbit roasted over the fire, they settled around the campfire talking. Suddenly Campbell rode into sight. His appearance was a shock to them all.

"What's he want?" hissed Meg.

"Easy," replied Peggy in a whisper, as she rose to her feet to greet him. "Remember he's a neighbour. They've been good to us."

"Nice evenin'," Campbell said in his Ontario country drawl. "I like the evenin's out here on the prairie. Gets calm and the wind drops. Sunsets are glorious." He slid off the back of his big horse and came to sit on a wooden box by the campfire.

Peggy and Campbell made small talk for a few minutes before he got to the point of his visit. "We're havin' a meetin' at our place tomorrow mornin', and I'd like your boy here, Jamie, to come along."

"What's the meeting about?" asked Peggy.

"About them Métis troublemakers," he said flatly.

"The Métis aren't troublemakers, sir," Jamie interjected pointedly. He could feel his stomach tighten into a knot. After what had happened, he felt he had to stand up for the Dauphins and all of the others.

Campbell stiffened. "They want us off this land, and they'll do anything to get rid of you and me and any of the settlers."

"They're honourable people."

"You were there. You saw those young fellows with their guns!"

"But you had guns, too!"

Campbell got to his feet. "We're just protectin' our own interest here, boy. This is our land now, and no Métis are goin' to take it back. If you can't see that they're plottin' against us English, then you're more of a fool than I thought."

To challenge an adult like this was hard. Jamie had got to his feet. His heart pounding, he said, "I'm not coming to the meeting."

Campbell regarded the boy with deep suspicion. "Are you soft on them Métis?"

"They've been good to us, Mr. Campbell."

There was a long pause as the farmer looked from one member of the Bains family to the other. "I don't like the sounds of this," he said finally. "If you choose the side of the Métis, there will be big trouble."

"They've never done anyone any harm," Jamie replied, trying hard to suppress the panic in his voice.

Campbell stared at him. His eyes narrowed and his mustache gave his face a hard frown. Then he walked to his horse and swung up into the saddle. "Suit yourself, boy," he said, looking down on them from on top of his horse. His voice had a threatening note. "But let me warn you. If you or your family get into trouble, don't come to me for help." Then he kicked the sides of his horse and the huge work animal lumbered out of their camp across the prairie.

Meg gave her brother a hug and said, "You're so strong, Jamie. I'm proud of you."

But the boy looked to his mother uneasily. Had he done the right thing?

Peggy watched Campbell's retreat without a word. Her face had a deeply worried expression.

# 11

Jamie continued to feel uneasy about the argument with Mr. Campbell. The next day as he worked he often looked to the west, across the prairie, expecting to see a group of angry farmers riding toward them. But they did not come.

The boy talked to Kate about what had happened, and she supported him. "They were out to get Louis. You stood up to Campbell. That was great," she said with enthusiasm.

But their mother shared Jamie's sense of unease. When they were alone, he asked her about the incident, and she replied, "We have to live with these people for a long time. I'm worried about what they will think about us and how they will treat us."

"Why do they hate the Métis so much?"

His mother thought for a moment before answering. "All over the world groups of people hate other groups for no other reason than they are different, or they think they are a threat, or maybe it's just that they have been taught to hate them. What you did was right, Jamie. We have to accept people and their differences, but what if our little community of families here on the prairie is divided over this, or we grow to hate each other? What will happen then?"

The boy thought about this as he went about his work. Like his mother, he worried about what might happen, but he knew deep down that he had to stand up for what was right even though there might be consequences that he did not like.

That morning Kate and Jamie went off to cut poles for the roof of the house. Louis arrived after lunch and helped them string the poles from the walls to the ridge log that went down the centre of the house.

Peggy continued with the ploughing. In the afternoon Jamie took over the job to give his mother a rest. He had come to enjoy ploughing. It was hard. He had to wrestle with the handles of the plough, pulling and tugging at them to keep the furrow straight, but he liked the smell of the fresh-turned earth and the feel of the cool soil as it was exposed to the sunlight.

It was while they were sitting around the campfire after supper that their mother announced that they were going to start planting. "We have ploughed about six acres," she explained. "It's late May, just about the right time to get in a crop. I just hope it ripens in time."

"How are we going to plant it, Mum?" asked Kate.

"Good question. We should have a harrow to level out the ground and cover up the seeds, but we don't have one. We'll have to do it by hand. Jamie do you think that you can make some rakes for us?"

Jamie had never worked on a farm, but he knew that a harrow was an implement with spikes that was dragged over ploughed ground to level it out and cover up the seeds. "Maybe I could rig up something that we could pull behind the buffalo pony," he said.

"Do you think you could do that?"

"I could try."

As the others continued to talk, Jamie tried to imagine how he could build a harrow out of their limited supply of material. Wood was something they had lots of. He could split one of the logs, then tie sticks or stakes onto the split side of the log that would act like the spikes of a harrow. The whole rig could be held in place with the other half of the log. It could be pulled with ropes leading to the saddle of the buffalo pony.

It was not exactly clear in his mind how he could make the harrow, and he knew there would be problems making it and using it, but anything would be better than trying to rake the seeds of grain into the ground by hand.

Peggy was explaining how the seeding would have to be done. "We'll have to make sure the seed is spread evenly across the field, and it will have to be covered by earth or the birds will eat it."

"I think we can make a harrow just as easily as making rakes," said Jamie. The boy explained briefly how he thought he could do it.

"Can I help?" asked Robbie.

"Sure. We'll work together on it."

Jamie got up the next morning and began gathering materials before they had breakfast. He was interested in finding out if he could build the harrow or not.

Louis came early, and the two girls worked with him to finish the roof. Everyone was anxious to move into the house as soon as possible. Living in the lean-to with no protection from the marauding black-flies and mosquitoes was intolerable.

Peggy began ploughing a patch of garden close to the house. The garden would be much smaller than the wheat field, but as Meg continued to remind them, it was just as important. This would be how they would get their vegetables for the winter.

Robbie and Jamie worked together building the harrow. First they selected a log about eight inches in diameter and about six feet long. The hardest part was splitting it in two. Jamie got the axe and drove it into the end of the log. Then, taking a hammer, he drove the axe farther and farther into the log. Slowly it began splitting, but the wood was wet, there were knots in it, and the grain was twisted. When the log finally separated and split apart, it was anything but the neat straight split that Jamie had imagined.

"What do you think, Robbie?" he asked.

"Maybe we should try another log," his brother replied.

"It will probably be as hard to split as this one. Let's see if we can get this to work."

They positioned about ten pieces of wood along the split log; these would act as the stakes or spikes that would drag along the ground like the prongs of a rake. They tied them into position and then tied the other side of the split log against the wood to hold them in place. All that was left to do was to tie ropes on either end of the log that would lead up to the horse's saddle. The whole process took no more than two hours.

Robbie was really impressed. "Boy, you're a real inventor, Jamie."

"No," he said, smiling at his little brother. "With most things you have to figure out what you need and then you can make something that does the job."

"Do you really think this will work?"

"It won't take long to find out."

They caught the buffalo pony, saddled him up, and brought him over to their new invention. They tied the ropes onto the saddle and dragged the harrow over to the field.

At first it was hopeless. As the pony dragged the harrow, Jamie couldn't hold the log in position; it rolled over and the stakes or spikes that were to dig into the ground were useless.

"We've got to have a handle on it in order for the wooden spikes to dig into the ground," Robbie concluded.

"Good thinking," said Jamie, and he really meant it.

They managed to rig up a handle so that the person driving the horse could position the harrow so the stakes dragged over the ground. Now they were ready to try again. Jamie held the reins to the pony in one hand and the handle of the harrow in the other.

"Gee up, come on." He shook the reins, and the pony began to move. Jamie held the harrow in position, and the stakes began to rake over the ploughed furrows.

"We've done it, Robbie," he said, laughing. "Go and tell mother."

The young boy took off like a rabbit. Robbie was so excited that everyone, including Louis, caught his enthusiasm and traipsed down to look at the invention. They were impressed. Robbie explained how they built the harrow and showed how easily they could replace any broken stakes. Finally he proudly told them how it was his idea to make the handle that controlled the harrow.

But it was not a complete success. Peggy recognized that the rig they had built was not nearly as good as a metal harrow, and they would still have to rake in much of the seed by hand, but she did not tell this to anyone. It was nice to see Robbie enjoy the attention. Her only comments were ones full of praise. "This is terrific, boys. It's going to save us a lot of backbreaking work."

For Jamie it was work in a different way. He walked behind the horse from one end of the field to the other, holding onto the handle of the harrow with one hand and the reins with the other. By mid-afternoon, he was totally exhausted and collapsed into the grass while the pony grazed beside him.

Robbie came running up excitedly. He flopped down beside his brother and asked breathlessly, "What's wrong, Jamie?"

"It's too much. I have to walk and steer the pony and hold that stupid handle for hours on end."

"Why don't I ride up on the horse's back and steer him, and you can look after the harrow."

Jamie thought about that for a moment. "Hey, that's a great idea, Robbie. Why didn't I think of that?" he said and laughed.

The partnership was terrific. The buffalo pony had wanted to break into a run all of the time. Jamie was having difficulty holding him back. This way Robbie could control the pony, and Jamie could concentrate on making sure that the stakes of the harrow were dragging through the ground as they should.

Robbie, for his part, had a great time. He loved being up on the pony's back even if the animal was plodding along through the field dragging a makeshift harrow. It didn't matter. As far as he was concerned, he was out riding on the prairie, as free as the wind.

By late afternoon they had harrowed the entire field once. The boys' mother came over to inspect their work. She stood, looking at the field thoughtfully, then picked up handfuls of dirt and threw them back.

"You boys did a good job, remarkable considering the tools you have. Still, this field is pretty rough. There is sod sticking through and bumps and hollows that should be levelled out. But we can't do any more. Tomorrow we have to start planting."

"Does that mean we don't do any more work with our harrow?" Robbie asked.

"You're going to be doing lots more of that. Don't worry."

"Good. I like doing it."

They unhitched the pony, hobbled him, and turned him loose. Then the three of them walked back to the house.

Louis and the girls had put sod on about half of one side of the roof. They were tired and dirty. When Peggy called to them to quit for the day, they did not need any encouragement.

Peggy talked casually as they walked back to the house. "It will be so good to move into the cabin. I'm sick and tired of camp life."

"Maybe we'll be able to get away from the bugs," said Robbie.

"Someday maybe we'll have a wooden house with a real kitchen and bedrooms and a parlour where we can sit and talk," she added, smiling to herself. For a long time a home of her own was only a remote possibility. Now, with hard work, it just might be possible.

Louis sat for a moment to drink a cup of tea and then said, "I must go."

"Are you sure you won't stay for supper?" asked Peggy.

"There is much I must do," he replied in English, but the others knew that Louis felt it would be wrong to eat their scarce supplies.

"I don't know how to thank you for what you have done for us," said Peggy.

He glanced at Meg and then said in English, "I'll help build the house, but the rest is up to you. Métis do not farm like this."

When he finished his tea, Louis stood up and scanned the horizon. He looked toward the west for a long time before saying simply, "They're coming."

"Who's coming?" asked Meg.

"Campbell and the others."

The members of the family got up to look. Three big horses with riders were approaching from the west. They were still too far away to make out clearly, but it had to be Campbell and the two young farmers, Albert and Frank.

"Maybe you should go before they arrive, Louis," Meg suggested gently.

Anger was just below the surface of the young Métis. "The English will not chase me off the prairie."

"But the last time you met them you —"

"They want me to run away! To vanish from the prairie like the buffalo." When he became angry, his English became more accented.

"There could be trouble."

"This is my home, Meg, and no one will come and drive me away!"

The Bains family and Louis stood and watched the three horses and their riders grow larger and larger as they neared the camp. Each of them felt a growing anxiety.

It was Mr. Campbell and the farmers, all right. They were riding on their big workhorses. The closer they came, the more determined they appeared. Albert was carrying his rifle in a long holster in his saddle. Finally the horses came into the camp.

"Well, ain't this just the cosy family," said Albert sarcastically. His thick broad shoulders gave him a powerful look.

The farmers stayed on their horses. This time there were no friendly greetings. Their faces were hard and determined. Frank seemed nervous. Campbell's sun-reddened face gave him an angry look.

"How can I help you, gentlemen?" asked Peggy, trying to stay calm.

"Strange. We were just on the way to the Dauphin place to find Louis," Campbell drawled.

"For why do you seek me?" Louis asked in broken English. He was wary and tense, turning from one to the other as if looking for a weakness.

"We had a meetin' of the neighbours yesterday at my place. It was decided that you were a dangerous man, Louis, and somethin' needs to be done about it."

Meg was incensed. "Who decided he was a dangerous man?"

"The other day he threatened us with a group of his friends, Miss Bains. All of those Métis were armed," Albert replied in a hostile voice. "Your brother and sister were there. Ask them."

"You had guns, too!" Kate shouted, very upset.

"What's wrong with you people?" demanded Frank impatiently. "Whose side are you on?"

"You were there, boy!" Albert pointed at Jamie. "Tell them how Louis threatened us!"

"You did a lot of threatening, too!" Jamie shot back, refusing to back down this time.

"He told us to get off Métis land! They were pointing guns at us!" Albert was shouting now.

"Gentlemen … gentlemen," Peggy said, trying to bring some reason back into the discussion. "It sounds like there were a lot of people doing the threatening. Maybe we should just calm down a little bit."

"I've had enough," said Albert. His eyes had a wild, angry look about them. "You tell them, Campbell!"

"It's like I said. We had a meetin' yesterday at my place, and it was decided that we had to do somethin'. We went into Portage la Prairie today and swore out a warrant for the arrest of Louis on account of his threatenin' us."

Louis was stunned. "A warrant? What does that mean?"

"They want to arrest you, Louis," Meg explained.

"I got the paper right here," Campbell added, reaching into his jacket pocket and bringing out an official-looking paper.

"Let me see that," said Peggy. She took the paper out of Campbell's hand and started to read it.

"Will you come with us peacefully, Louis, or do we have to take you in by force?"

Louis was like a trapped fox. "What chance will I have before an English judge?" he said, looking from Peggy to Meg to Campbell and back again.

"You can't do that!" Meg exclaimed irately.

"We've already done it, miss."

Albert sneered at Meg. "You're altogether too friendly with these Métis."

"You'd be better off if you were a little friendlier," she shouted in reply.

"There can be no friendship between Métis and English."

"That's where you're dead wrong, Albert!" Meg replied. "Now, take your stupid warrant and get out of here!"

"We're goin' nowhere unless we have Louis as our prisoner!"

"We were ordered by the court to bring him in," Campbell repeated.

Suddenly Louis made his decision. He was standing between Meg and Peggy. He ducked behind them and sprinted for his pony that was by the cart. He swept the reins up in his hand and vaulted into the saddle.

"He's makin' a run for it!" Frank shouted.

"Head him off!" ordered Campbell.

Frank kicked the sides of his horse. The big lumbering animal moved slowly.

Kate was shouting, "Go, Louis!" Robbie joined in the yelling.

Jamie saw Albert pull the long rifle from the holster on his saddle. He raised it to his shoulder.

Louis jerked the reins, and his pony leaped into a gallop. He moulded himself to the back of his horse.

Albert was taking careful aim at the fleeing figure. Jamie threw himself at his big horse. The animal shied back. The rifle flew up and Albert lost his aim. Louis' horse thundered out of the camp as he headed toward the line of trees in the distance.

"Damn you, boy! I had a clear shot at him."

"He's getting away!" Frank shouted. He spurred after him, but within moments Louis' fleet pony had left the lumbering workhorse far behind.

"You let him get away!" Albert cried, pointing at Jamie. He was in a rage.

"There'll be no shooting here!" Peggy exclaimed. "No matter what he did, Louis does not deserve to be shot!"

"You'll pay for this! You'll pay. Just wait and see!"

"Come on!" Campbell shouted. "Maybe we can get him down at his father's place."

The three farmers rode their horses as fast as they would go, leaving the members of the Bains family in stunned silence.

*Travelling to the new province of Manitoba in the 1870s was difficult. From Ontario, most people travelled by train through Chicago and St. Paul, Minnesota, to Fisher's Landing on the Red River and down the Red to Winnipeg aboard steamboats such as the Selkirk, shown here.*
National Archives of Canada, PA 74666.

*Main Street, Winnipeg in 1876 when the city had little more than 5,000 inhabitants.*
National Archives of Canada, C 22617.

*Before settlement, the treeless prairie stretched from the Red River Valley to the Rocky Mountains. The only features that broke the landscape were river valleys, lined with oak and poplar trees. In 1872 the prairie was opened for homesteading. Any head of a family, over the age of 21, was entitled to a quarter section of land by paying a filing fee of $10. It was only after the railway arrived in 1881 that large numbers of settlers came to Manitoba and the lands further west.*
National Archives of Canada, PA 11756.

*The Red River cart, pulled by an ox, was the most common form of transportation across the Canadian west before the railway. Carts, made out of wood and leather, could carry huge loads.*
National Archives of Canada, PA 61689.

*The Métis, a mixed race of French and Indian people, made up the majority of the population in Manitoba prior to 1870. They spoke their own dialect of French and had a well-developed culture and social life. The Métis were great horsemen. They prided themselves on their independence and* joie de vivre. *This illustration, by the Canadian artist Charles Jefferys, shows a Métis horse race outside the walls of Fort Garry.*
Charles Jefferys Collection, National Archives of Canada, C 73598.

*Métis life revolved around the buffalo. Twice a year the hunters and their families went onto the prairie to hunt buffalo and render the meat into pemmican, used in the fur trade. By the mid-1870s the buffalo became increasingly scarce and finally disappeared. This led to a serious crisis for the Métis.*
Manitoba Museum of Man and Nature.

*Métis men and women, dressed for a special occasion.*
National Archives of Canada, C 79642.

*This hunter wears a typical Métis outfit of colourful shirt, coat and sash.
He has a muzzle-loaded musket.*
National Archives of Canada, C-79643.

*Louis Riel was the leader of the Métis people in both the Red River Rebellion of 1870 and the North-West Rebellion of 1885. He was hung for treason on November 16, 1885 in Regina.*
National Archives of Canada, C 52177.

*The Métis farmed narrow strips of land that went back from the river. There they built their homes, tended their gardens and looked after their cattle. Farming was just a sideline for them. Before the settlement of the prairies, Métis families supported themselves in the buffalo hunt or by transporting goods by Red River carts along the prairie trails.*
National Archives of Canada, C 61461.

*Many Indian people continued to live a nomadic life on the prairies in the 1870s.*
National Archives of Canada, PA 50799.

*Weddings were great social occasions for the Métis. Fiddlers played non-stop for hours while men and women danced the Red River jig until they were exhausted. This picture, done by an amateur artist, has an odd perspective, but it captures the spirit of the event.*
Minnesota Historical Society. Artist: Corp. Louis Voelkerer

*As homesteaders moved onto the prairies, shelter was a major problem. There was little wood for construction, it was expensive and often had to be hauled long distances. The sod hut was the perfect solution. Thick, earthen walls gave warmth in winter, protection against the howling wind, could be built with materials close at hand and cost no more than the labour to build them.*
National Archives of Canada, PA 73668.

*Buffalo bones covered the prairie when the homesteaders first arrived. They could be either burned or sold for fertilizer. Dried buffalo dung also provided a great fuel for cooking fires.*
National Archives of Canada, C 5123.

*For the homesteader, breaking the virgin prairie sod and planting that first crop were the most important tasks. Oxen were preferred by many farmers. They were slow but easy to handle and very strong.*
National Archives of Canada, PA 200771.

*Everyone had to work, on the farm. Boys and girls as young as nine and ten handled horses, worked in the fields, cared for animals and did chores around the house.*
National Archives of Canada, PA 117285.

*Once the hay or grain was ripe it was cut with a scythe, like the one that this man is using. In the latter part of the nineteenth and the twentieth centuries various farm machines such as mechanized mowers, reapers and binders were introduced.*
National Archives of Canada, PA 60748.

*Wheat soon became the most valuable crop on the prairies. Once cut it was tied into bundles and stooked in order to dry. Finally, it was threshed by knocking the grain kernels off the stock. In the nineteenth century this was usually done with flails. Later crews used huge threshing machines. Today the whole process, from mowing the wheat to threshing, is done with combines.*
National Archives of Canada, PA 60746.

*A successful harvest was absolutely essential to the survival of the homestead. Everybody pitched in to work.*
National Archives of Canada, PA 11571.

*Fires and grasshoppers could be disasterous to the prairie farm. The plowed land in the foreground of this picture is a firebreak protecting the grain and hay in the field behind. Raging prairie firestorms could leap over a firebreak even this wide and farmers had to be vigilant.*
National Archives of Canada, PA 11412.

*Settlers often burned firebreaks around their fields. When a prairie fire burned up to the firebreak it would die because it had no fuel to feed it.*
National Archives of Canada, PA 18309.

*Men and women worked together on Canadian farms to make their enterprise a success. The usual division of labour was that men worked in the fields and with the large animals, while women worked around the house, tended the garden and looked after the smaller animals such as the chickens. When the men were absent, women and children did all of the work on the farm.*
National Archives of Canada, PA 125724.

*Life for the settlers on the Canadian prairies was never easy. Even after a family gathered together enough money to build a house, they faced loneliness, isolation and hard work.*

National Archives of Canada, C 22394.

*Settlers came to the prairies from around the world, determined to forge a new life in a harsh land. They were driven by their dreams, and they were sustained by their hard work, their willingness to help each other and their strong spirit. Some failed, but many reaped the rewards of those years of hardship by turning the prairies into a place that is called "the bread basket of the world."*

National Archives of Canada, PA 200772.

*Plough*

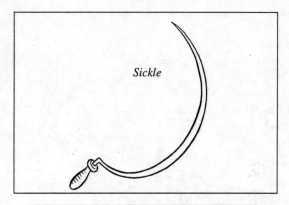

*Sickle*

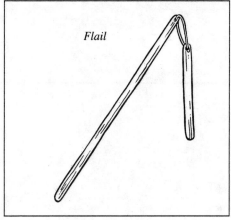

*Flail*

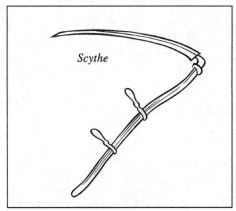

*Scythe*

*Harrow*

# 12

Supper that night was a quiet affair. Everyone was worried about Louis. Had he escaped? Were the angry farmers hot on his trail? They just did not know.

All evening long one or the other of them would get up and look across the prairie, half expecting to see the farmers or Louis in the distance, but the place was empty of life. After a spectacular sunset, they lit the smudge pots and climbed under the blankets in the lean-to.

Robbie and Kate had already drifted off to sleep when Jamie asked the question on everyone's mind.

"What do you think will happen to Louis?"

"They had better not hurt him," said Meg, into the gathering darkness.

"Albert is such a rigid and unforgiving man. I worry about what he might do," whispered Peggy, so she would not wake the younger children.

They listened to the night sounds for a moment, and then Jamie spoke again, "Albert said that he was going to get me because I spoiled his aim."

"It's just as well you did, Jamie, or there would be murder on his hands."

"As long as Louis is all right …" Meg's words trailed off into the night.

Overhead the stars gleamed like brilliant pinpoints of light in a cloudless sky. The Milky Way was a river of stars flowing across the sky from north to south. As they lay, listening and watching, a three-quarter moon slowly rose over the eastern horizon casting a pale light over the prairie grasslands. An owl hooted from a distance, crickets sang in an unbroken chorus, and a soft breeze stirred the leaves of the oak tree overhead.

Finally Peggy spoke into the darkness. "We're here to build a new life on the prairies, but it seems that old hatreds will not stop. I just hope that they will not consume us all." Her words were spoken to the stars. The others were fast asleep.

The next morning Peggy got the family up before dawn and served them a big breakfast of oatmeal. Meg moped around the campsite, buried in her own thoughts. The younger children were tired. The long hours of hard work were wearing them down. They sat around the campfire, half dozing and huddling into their clothes to keep warm in the cool morning air.

Peggy tried to put the problems of Louis behind them. "This should be a day of celebration. Finally we're ready to start the planting."

"Do we have to?" Kate grumbled.

Peggy tried her most optimistic tone. "We've got to get our crops in the ground so they ripen in time. One or two more days of work, and then we will be able to get some rest."

"But Mother, that's what you always say."

"I promise, Kate. We'll do all the planting and finish the house, and then we'll take two days to do something completely different. All right?"

Jamie got up and stretched. "Come on, Robbie. You're going to ride the buffalo pony all day today."

Peggy got the precious bag of Red Fife wheat seed that she had brought all the way from Ontario. Carefully they carried it over to the field. Then she organized the work.

"We have to be careful to spread the seed as evenly as possible. There should be enough to cover the field. We have to spread it by hand, and then the boys will work it into the ground with their harrow."

Meg and Kate started the job of spreading the seeds. It was not difficult, but Peggy worried about it constantly. A little more here, a little less there. She spread seeds herself, but also carried a shovel in her hands to break up big pieces of earth.

Before they started the boys had to replace two broken stakes in their harrow. Jamie also decided to sharpen the stakes so they would make a smaller furrow as they dragged across the ground. It was mid-morning before they were ready to begin, and the girls had already seeded about a third of the field.

Robbie rode the pony out onto the field. Jamie positioned the handle so the stakes would drag through the ground, waved his hand to his brother to indicate he was ready, and off they went with the buffalo pony pulling their makeshift rig across the broken, ploughed land. Back and forth they went across the field, working the seeds into the ground with their harrow.

By the time the sun reached its highest point in the sky, they were well over half finished seeding the wheat field. They stopped for a quick lunch, and then went right back to work again.

An hour later Meg, Kate, and Peggy were finished the field and had emptied the bag of seed. The three of them lay down in the long grass and watched the boys work the field with their harrow.

"Robbie really likes riding that horse," said Peggy. "When we came here, I was worried about him but look at him now."

They rested for a few minutes, and then Meg got them going again. "Let's get cracking on that garden. It's as important as the wheat field."

They let the boys finish the harrowing of the field and headed back to the camp. Meg rummaged around in the cart and found the seeds they had bought in Winnipeg. They spread them out in a row: potatoes, squash, carrots, turnip, corn, peas, beans, and pumpkin.

"If every one of these crops come in, we'll eat like kings over the winter," said Peggy with a smile.

The vegetable garden was a little more than an acre in size. It did not look very big in comparison with the wheat field, but they had to plant each of these seeds individually.

They started with the potatoes and carefully laid each seed potato into the bottom of the furrow. Then one of them spread about an inch of dirt over the top of the seeds with the shovel. They planted three rows of potatoes before they finished the seed. Then they moved on to plant beans.

The boys came and joined them after they had finished harrowing the wheat field. Under Peggy's direction they began seeding rows of corn, squash, peas, carrots, beans, turnips, and then pumpkins.

By late afternoon they were already finished their seeding. The whole family went back to the camp and started a fire to boil water for tea. They were all very tired, and their backs ached from bending over as they planted the vegetable seeds, but each of them felt a real sense of accomplishment in having finally completed the planting.

"That didn't take very long," said Kate.

"Seeding always goes quickly," replied Peggy. "It's preparing the ground that takes the time."

Before the water had boiled, Meg got to her feet and walked a few yards away from the camp to scan the horizon. She had been quiet all day. The others exchanged worried glances as they watched her.

When she came back to the fire, Jamie asked, "Do you want me to take the pony and go and look for him, Meg?"

She gave her brother a weak smile and said, "I'm not worried about him. Louis can look after himself. It's …" The words petered out before she could form them in her mind.

What was between Meg and Louis? No one knew for sure, but Peggy could guess. Many years before, when she courted her husband Angus, she felt that sense of loss and longing whenever he was not around. She knew that there was nothing she could say that would make Meg feel any better and so she remained silent.

But Louis did come. That evening as they sat around the fire finishing their supper Meg heard hooves pounding on the prairie, and the young Métis galloped into camp on his bay pony. He had a buckskin jacket over his shirt and heavy saddlebags hung from his horse.

Meg rushed to him as he tied his horse up to the wheel of the Red River cart.

"I was afraid that they might catch you," she said, touching his arm tenderly.

He smiled at her. "Those farmers are the slowest things moving on the prairie," he replied in French. Louis studied the horizon to make sure there were no horsemen before he joined the others at the fire. "I led them a merry dance before I lost them in the trees down by the river."

"It's just so good to see you." Meg could not suppress her smiles.

"Have they come back here?"

"No and they better not come, or I'll put them in their place."

"I came to thank you," Louis said. "No matter what I said about the English, the Bainses have been true friends to me and the Métis people." He looked handsome with his long dark hair and flashing, quick eyes.

"Thank you," said Peggy quietly. "We will honour your friendship, Louis."

"I must go. My trail will take me long way."

"Where are you going?" Kate asked.

He looked at the young girl and smiled but said nothing. The less they knew the better. As he got up to leave, Meg grasped his hand. "Walk with me," she said simply.

The two walked slowly out onto the prairie. The sun was beginning to set, streaking the western sky with orange, yellow, and pink colours. They talked intently, looking deeply into each other's eyes.

When they returned Louis gathered the reins and mounted his horse. *"Au revoir,"* he shouted to the group gathered around the fire.

Then, completely unexpectedly, he leaned out of his saddle, and kissed Meg on the cheek. *"Au revoir,"* he shouted again, and his horse galloped out of camp. Soon he was only a shadow against the western sky.

The visit changed Meg's mood completely. Now she hummed to herself happily and chatted away to anyone who would listen. The next morning she was the first one out of bed. She made porridge and was anxious to get working.

The last big job to complete the house was finishing the roof. Jamie got the sled, hitched it to the pony, and they went out onto the prairie to cut sod. Meg worked with him, and they laboriously cut the squares of sod with the shovel, pulled them from their roots, and stacked them on the sled. When it was full, Robbie insisted on climbing into the saddle and riding the pony back to the house while the others walked.

Louis had made a rough ladder when he worked on the roof, and they used it to carry the sod pieces up and put them in place. By mid-morning they had finished one side of the roof and were beginning to work on the other.

"Is this sod really going to keep out the rain?" Robbie asked as they took a break. "It's really just dirt with some grass growing on it."

The boy's mother shrugged. "I've never lived in a sod house," she said. "I don't know, but what we really have to think about is the winter. It gets bitterly cold out here. This sod house is going to be warmer than anything else that we could build because the walls and roof are so thick."

They worked hard all afternoon, and by supper time Jamie placed the last piece of sod onto the roof. The boy climbed down to the ground and joined the others, who were admiring their new home. It was still unfinished. Spaces had been left for the windows and door until they could get the money to buy them in town, but the sod hut looked livable.

"Come on inside," said Kate, leading them through the empty doorway.

The members of the Bains family stood in the middle of the hut looking at the rough walls and the dirt floor. Light came through the walls in a dozen places. Tufts of grass poked out into the room. The floor was uneven and marked with scars from the shovel.

"I don't think you could call this the lap of luxury, but it's home," Peggy said, smiling broadly.

Meg's optimism matched her mother's. "Maybe we can get some boards and put them on the floor. With a couple of windows and a door, it will be as cosy as any place in Manitoba."

"What about a stove?" asked Jamie. "It's going to be mighty cold this winter without one."

Peggy laughed. "The money for a stove is out in the field growing as we talk about it. Come on. We've slept in that lean-to for the last night. Let's get our things and move in!"

They gathered all of their belongs together, loaded them onto the sled, and dragged it across to the new sod house. Peggy sang a song about the Red River Valley as she hung cloth across the window and door openings to keep the insects out while the others carried their possessions into the

house. She seemed happier than at any time since they had
arrived at their farm.

All evening they puttered around the house trying to find
places for the few things that they owned. As it darkened,
they lit two of their precious candles so they could see. There
were no tables; they had only the boxes that they used to store
their possessions, which doubled as makeshift chairs. The
two boys went out and cut some prairie grass with their sickle
and lay it on the floor in one corner of the house for bedding.
That would have to do until they had time to make real beds.

For Peggy, putting up the family pictures was the thing
that converted the sod hut into a home. She found her three
precious photographs carefully wrapped in an old cloth, between some bedding, in the most sturdy box they had brought
from Ontario. Carefully she brought them out and lay them
beside a candle so she could see them.

There was the photograph of John and Meg taken in front
of their small cottage in Ottawa just before they left on the
log raft for Quebec City. Meg looked so young and fresh.
John was standing proudly like an independent young man
about to go off and seek his fortune. That day, two summers
before, was the last time she had seen her oldest son.

The most precious picture she owned was the one of her
husband, Angus. It was taken in a photographer's studio a
month before he went into the logging shanty that last season.
He was a strong, squarely built man with a shock of dark hair.
In the picture Peggy could see the good humour just behind
his handsome blue eyes. She missed him more than she could
describe.

The third picture had been taken on their wedding day
many years before. The photograph was old and beginning to
curl around the edges. Peggy and Angus were sitting stiffly in
an uncomfortable wooden settee, but they were smiling at

each other, so much in love and excited about the life that they were going to build together.

She studied the pictures for a long time and was not aware that tears were flowing down her cheeks until she looked up, searching for the best place to hang them. Quickly she wiped the tears away before the children could notice.

Peggy found the spot for the pictures in a corner of the hut and propped them up in among the roots and sticks that were hanging from the dirt walls. That would have to do until they were more settled.

Everyone stayed up late, fussing around in the new home until the candles burned down and started to flicker. Tomorrow was going to be a day off, and they would have the luxury of sleeping in.

In the morning Peggy got up as the sun was coming over the horizon. She walked over to the campsite and boiled some water over the fire for tea. She had set aside a book the night before and found a comfortable place in the sun to read it. Books were the one luxury they had allowed themselves, and she enjoyed the reading time immensely.

About two hours later, Meg got up, and they had some breakfast together. It was as they were finishing that Meg scanned the horizon and saw Mr. Campbell riding his big horse toward them.

"What does he want?" Meg asked anxiously.

"Try to be polite."

"I'm not going to be polite after what he did to Louis."

"Just try, that's all."

The big horse lumbered along, and finally Campbell made it to the camp. The farmer slid to the ground and joined the two women.

"Mornin' ladies, mornin'. I see you've got that sod house finished. Looks like a fair job."

"It'll be warm next winter," replied Peggy in a noncommittal way.

"I daresay that's the truth. You need to be close to the ground in winter in these parts."

"I don't imagine you came to talk to us about our house." Peggy was direct and to the point.

Campbell shifted uneasily. "Well, no," he admitted.

"You should never have taken the warrant out against Louis," said Meg angrily.

"It's not good for neighbours to fight," he said, avoiding Meg's point. "Ruby was askin' about you. There's another new family that's moved in close to us, and Ruby figured that it would be good if you could come over this afternoon and meet them."

"What about the warrant, Mr. Campbell?" Meg demanded.

"That's not up to us. It was the court that issued the warrant."

"But you and Albert and Frank were the ones trying to arrest him!"

"Well, that Albert, he goes a little overboard."

"But you were part of it, too!"

"I'm just tryin' to be a good neighbour here. Ruby insisted that I come over and invite you. 'That Peggy's a widow woman,' is what Ruby said. 'She's got a hard row to hoe. Now, you head on over there, and invite her and her family to come for tea and to meet the neighbours.' That's what Ruby said."

Peggy had been silent, listening to what Campbell had to say. When she spoke, it was with a clear and determined focus. "That's kind of Ruby, and I would like to meet the new neighbours, but I'm not going to go to your place if it is just another chance to condemn Louis and the Métis people. A school for the children is what I want to talk about. If you promise to talk about a school, I'll be happy to come."

"Schools for the young ones? That's a perfect thing to talk about. You bring your brood over this afternoon, and we'll talk about schools for sure."

He set the time for them to come, and then headed back on his horse across the prairie toward his place.

# 13

I'm not going. That's all there is to it," said Meg angrily, once Campbell was out of earshot.

Peggy was thoughtful. "I wonder why they have invited us," she said. "It's not just to meet the new neighbours. We've made it pretty clear that we don't support their efforts to get Louis arrested."

"They think they can trick us into telling them where Louis has gone."

"It could be that, or maybe they want to try and persuade us that we are wrong to support the Métis. Perhaps it's simply that Ruby insisted on us being invited."

"Well, I won't sit around and talk about Louis or condemn the Métis people."

"We need to know what they're thinking, Meg," said Peggy. "Anyway I think it's important to try and get a school organized for the fall."

"You go if you want, Mother, but I'm not going!" Meg declared emphatically and walked away in order to terminate the conversation.

The others did not get up until late in the morning. Over breakfast Peggy announced to them that they would be visiting the Campbells that afternoon. The response she got was near rebellion. Both Kate and Jamie said flatly that they were not going to go.

"Well then I'll just have to go myself," Peggy replied. "I'm determined that we have a school by this fall, and we need our neighbours to make that happen."

There were groans and complaints from the kids, but as she was getting ready to leave early in the afternoon, Jamie, Kate, and Robbie agreed to accompany her. "At least they have good food," was Robbie's comment.

But Meg would not relent. "There is no way I'm going to listen to those people."

"All right," said her mother. "You're almost a grown woman. You decide for yourself."

They took their time getting dressed in their best outfits, and then Kate and Peggy set off walking while Robbie and Jamie rode the buffalo pony. The boys ranged a long way ahead of the others, exploring the landscape and enjoying the freedom of riding beneath the huge prairie sky. After a while, Jamie got dropped on the trail and let his younger brother ride the pony by himself while he walked with the others.

The horse and rider galloped on ahead and then circled back. They scared rabbits. A prairie chicken ran away, and gophers darted back into their holes to avoid the sharp hooves. Peggy could only marvel at how her youngest son was developing into a strong, resourceful boy.

When the Bains family arrived at the Campbell place, other people were already there. Frank and Albert, dressed in their Sunday clothes, were seated in the garden, eating big pieces of cake and drinking tea. Another man and woman sat with them. The woman, in her mid-twenties, was cradling a baby in her arms while her husband, about eight years older, watched possessively. They were country people, with sun-reddened faces and hands hardened from years of work.

The group was huddled next to the house, trying to keep out of the wind and sun. The table, laden with delicious-looking food, was covered with a bright red checkered table-cloth.

As they arrived, Ruby rushed out of the house to greet them followed by her husband.

"Peggy, so good to see you, welcome." As the big woman laughed, her whole body shook. "I see you brought the three young, hungry ones, but where is Meg?"

"She decided to stay at home and do a few chores."

"The bachelors will be disappointed with that, but you're just in time for the cake. Help yourself, please." With Ruby, everyone was made to feel at home.

More chairs were brought out of the house by the bachelors and put around the big table that lay in the shade of the house. Introductions were made to the new settlers, a young couple by the name of Graham who came from the St. Mary's area of southwestern Ontario. The women fussed over the new baby, asked about their trip out to Manitoba and the location of their homestead. The mother explained that they had two other children, five and six years of age, who were playing with the Campbell kids.

The group of adults settled on the chairs in a circle. Peggy helped Ruby bring food and a big pot of fresh tea out into the garden, and they joined the others. It was Frank who asked about Meg, and Peggy had to give excuses again.

The young farmer persisted. "I expect Meg will be looking for her own place to live now that you have about finished buildin' that sod house of yours," as he laughed his thin frame shook and his mustache turned up into a smile.

Peggy was not sure what he was saying. "Well, no," she replied.

"A young, attractive woman like that is not about to be single for long."

Peggy gave him a frosty smile, and said, "One thing you will learn about Meg is that she makes her own decisions, and it will be an unusual man who will win her hand."

Over fresh tea and cake the adults began talking seriously. Peggy had come to discuss the school, and she was not to be put off. "I think that it is very important that we have a school organized for the children as soon as possible," she proposed. "It is almost June. That doesn't leave us much time if we want to start school right after the harvest."

"It'll be too difficult," replied Frank. "We will have to have a building. There is no money for a teacher."

"With all respect, sir, you don't have children, so it's not important to you," Peggy said bluntly. "Even though we are isolated, our children have to have an education. What do you think, Ruby?"

The big woman glanced uneasily at her husband. "They need their readin' and writin'. No doubt about that. But as I explained before we don't have enough children."

"Are you sure about that, Ruby?"

"I wrote the government in Winnipeg myself. They said we have to have fifteen children before they give us any funds. I've got four kids, there are three in the Bains family and two school-aged Graham children. That makes nine we've got now, but that's still not enough."

"Well, there are more than fifteen children in the neighbourhood," Peggy said calmly.

"Who?" "Where?" The others were puzzled.

"There are Métis families living down by the river who don't have a school. The Dauphins have four and then there are more children living to the east of them. We could have a lot of kids for the school."

There was a moment of shocked silence as the others took in what was being proposed. Peggy knew that this was a radical, unacceptable idea, but she was determined to get a school for her children even if the others thought her solution was inappropriate.

"But they are Catholic and French," said Albert. "They should have their own schools."

"Why? They have children that need education, the same as us. Why shouldn't they all go to the same school?"

"But it's not done," Albert replied. "Catholics shouldn't go to school with Protestant children."

"But we all live out here in isolation. We don't have the luxury to have two schools."

"But this is a Protestant country. Those Métis ... why they're only a little above the Indians."

Peggy stiffened and said, "What's wrong with the Indians, sir?" She knew that she was getting into more trouble all the time, but she would not back down.

Mr. Campbell tried to be jovial in an attempt to head off an argument. "Well, Peggy, you have to admit that they just are not civilized."

"Are we any more civilized?"

"That's one thing that I will not put up with," said Albert stubbornly. "For us to educate the Métis and the Indians would be wrong. If the French and the Catholics want their schools, then they can build them and pay for them by themselves."

"We've come and taken their land. The least we can do is share our education with them."

It was an awkward moment, and Ruby tried to smooth out the differences. "I don't see how we can do anything about a school. At least not this year. Let's have some more tea, folks. There's lots more cake. I know these young men are all hungry for cake."

Peggy grew quiet. She had hoped that they could find a friendly solution to the issue of the school, but just the opposite had happened. Now the neighbours would look at the Bains family as people with crazy ideas about Métis and Indians. How could it ever be patched up now?

Albert, his face red with anger, sat stiffly across from her saying nothing. It was clear from his every motion that he was so furious that he did not trust himself to speak.

Later in the afternoon, as they prepared to leave, Albert cornered Jamie over by the food table where the others could not hear. "Looks like you and your family have taken the side of the Métis," he whispered.

Jamie was confused. "What do you mean?"

"We're watchin' you, boy. I know that you were the one who helped Louis Dauphin escape. If you make any attempt to help that no good Métis again, then I can assure you that you'll be goin' to jail along with him. Remember that. It'll be jail or somethin' even worse than jail." The hatred in Albert's face made Jamie draw back in fear.

As the Bains family was leaving, Ruby drew Peggy aside. "You should drop this talk about the Métis. The men will never accept it." She put her arm around her shoulder to make her feel better.

"We can't let this happen, Ruby," Peggy said. It's up to us to bring neighbours together," but the big woman only smiled grimly and went to say her goodbyes to the others who were leaving.

When they got back home, Peggy explained to Meg what had happened. "It was terrible," she concluded. "Maybe you were right, and we shouldn't have gone."

"Didn't I tell you?"

"But what are we going to do about the school? The three young ones need more education. We can't let these prejudices stand in our way."

"Those people are not going to change, Mother."

"I just hope you're wrong."

That night, after supper, the Bains family were huddling around candles in the new sod hut reading or doing chores. Peggy set down her mending and listened. "Rain," she said softly.

"Are you sure?" asked Meg.

Jamie went to the door and pulled back the cloth they were using to keep out the insects. A soft rain was falling. Already the grass was wet with a good soaking rain.

Peggy smiled and said, "That's what we need more than anything else. Lots of steady rain."

It rained all night and by morning the leaks came through the sod roof in a dozen places. Kate was awakened by a drip that landed right in her face, and Meg felt damp through the blankets down by her feet. Their mother just laughed.

"The wheat crop and vegetables are dying of thirst. It's the best thing for us," she said. We need this rain desperately." Peggy's spirits had lifted with the rain.

It rained all that day and into the next night. By the time it stopped, the interior of the house was almost as damp as it was outside, but Peggy remained in high spirits.

There was not much work that could be done so Jamie, Kate, and Robbie went out to set snares for rabbits. Afterwards they went down to the marsh to look at the ducks. There was a whole group of mallards cruising on the water. Many of them were small, recently hatched ducklings.

Robbie insisted on staying to watch the young brood. He was fascinated with birds of all kinds and would have stayed there for hours if his older brother and sister had not grown impatient and insisted on leaving.

It was as they were walking back home, leading the buffalo pony, that they spotted an Indian teepee near a clump of trees close to the marsh. A small band was huddled around a campfire.

"What are we going to do?" asked Robbie with panic in his voice.

"Maybe they won't see us," whispered Jamie. They had seen lots of Indians since they had been in Manitoba but had never come across any on the open prairie. They had heard many stories about the Indian wars and knew that to the south of them the Sioux Nation was sporadically waging war against the U.S. Cavalry.

Jamie climbed up into the saddle of the buffalo pony, Kate came up behind him with Robbie in front. It was a heavy load for the pony, but if they had to make a run for it, they might have a chance.

But just as they urged the pony into a trot, an Indian appeared in front of them. He was mounted bareback on a spotted pony. His shiny black hair was braided neatly down the back of his head, and two eagle feathers were stuck into it. He wore a vest of doe skin, blue woolen pants, and beautifully decorated moccasins. Held in front of him was a Winchester repeater rifle. If he chose to attack them, they would not have a chance.

On second glance they saw that the Indian was not a man at all but a boy about fourteen years of age. He was smiling and holding his hand up, with an open palm toward them in the Plains' Indian sign of peace.

Jamie reined in the pony, and they tried to talk to the Indian first in French and then in English but with no success. The Indian boy rubbed his belly.

"Hungry?" asked Kate, and she made a motion of feeding herself.

He nodded his head enthusiastically.

"Come on," Kate said. She waved to him, and they started to head back to their homestead.

The Indian followed them, but he was motioning. "He wants you to ride with him, Kate," said Robbie.

"I'm not going to do that."

But she did not have a choice. The Indian kicked his pony, and in a moment he had caught up to them. He reached over, grabbed Kate around the waist, and deftly pulled her off the buffalo pony and onto his own horse. At the same time, he whooped and forced his horse into a gallop. Kate was absolutely petrified. She thought that she might be carried off over the prairie and be the captive of an Indian band forever.

Jamie panicked. He booted the buffalo pony hard, and his horse broke into a fast gallop. In a moment they had caught up to the Indian horse, but just as he came abreast of him the Indian boy turned and smiled at them happily. It was a game that he was playing.

In that instant Kate understood and got caught up in the game. She held on tight to the Indian boy, and the two horses raced together across the prairie. All four of them were whooping and yelling. It took only minutes for the two horses to arrive back at the Bainses' homestead.

Peggy and Meg were startled to see the two horses come thundering across the prairie and even more astounded to find that Kate was riding behind an Indian boy dressed for the hunt. But they reined in, and the four of them slid off their horses close to the campfire.

"He's hungry," Kate explained. "So we brought him home."

The Indian boy made it clear by pointing and gesturing that what he wanted was porridge, and so Peggy made up a big batch of the gooey stuff even though it was late in the afternoon. The boy sat and watched the cooking until it was finished. Then Kate served him a big bowl, which he dug into with contented sounds. He licked the bowl right down to the last morsel, stood up and pointed at the sack of cereal.

"He wants to take some oats home with him," said Kate, who seemed to pick up instinctively what he was saying.

"We can give him a little, but we need the rest for ourselves."

They separated out about a pound of the dry oats into a small cloth bag and gave it to the Indian boy. He smiled broadly, held his hand up in the sign of peace again, and in a moment had mounted his pony and disappeared back the way they had come.

"Strange behavior," Robbie commented, as he watched him go.

"Maybe the Indians are starving," replied his mother. "They lived off the buffalo, and now that they have disappeared, all they have to eat is small game."

It was two days later when the Indian boy suddenly reappeared in their camp riding his pony. He had four large ducks tied together with a thong which he presented to Peggy and Kate. Then, as quickly as he had appeared, he turned his horse and rode out of the camp.

That night the Bains family feasted on wild roast duck slowly turned on a spit over the fire. It was one of the most delicious meals that any of them had ever eaten.

The days passed with few incidents. Now that the planting was completed they had more time to themselves. Jamie and Kate turned to hunting to provide fresh meat for the family. Often they would meet the Indian boy and the three would ride and hunt. Robbie read his books, set snares, and studied the birds. Peggy worked around the sod hut, trying to make it into a real home while Meg spent hours watching the skyline to the west, waiting for the return of a lone horseman.

One day, about a week after they had finished the planting, Peggy came into the hut before breakfast, filled with excitement. The wheat had come up. Everyone had to go and see.

Their mother treated it like a triumph. The wheat stood an inch tall, like a fresh green fuzz that covered the black soil of the wheat field. Nothing could have made her happier.

As the end of June approached, the days were so long that the family went to bed before the sun set and got up after it had risen. The black flies disappeared, and there were fewer mosquitoes, leaving only the deer flies to bother them. As the days merged into July, it became hotter and hotter as the sun beat down relentlessly on the prairie. And every day the wheat in the field and the vegetables in the garden grew higher and higher.

They worked on a variety of chores. They stopped up all of the holes in the walls of the house and patched the leaks in the roof as best they could. They watered the vegetable garden, checked the snares, cooked over the open fire, and watched the crop grow steadily higher. And every day Meg scanned the horizon, waiting and watching.

# 14

The summer equinox had come and gone, and the hot weather descended. The spring rains slowed and the sun baked the land. Wild prairie grass slowly turned from green to yellow. The horses grew fat from endless days of grazing. Young ducklings had learned to fly, and there were weeks when it seemed they would be overrun by gophers and rabbits.

One hot summer day Jamie and Kate were hitching the cart to Baby so they could haul water to the vegetable garden when Robbie came running up with the news that Monsieur Dauphin was coming. "Go and tell Mother and Meg," Jamie told him, and the boy took off on a run toward the house.

*"Bonjour, Kat'leen, Jamie, comment ça va?"* was the greeting of the Métis as he rode up on his horse.

*"Ça va bien,"* Kate answered, switching easily into French.

"It is surely a fine summer day. A day when it is good to be alive and free and riding on the prairie." Dauphin laughed in his good-natured way. "How is that buffalo pony of yours?"

Kate bubbled over with enthusiasm. "He's wonderful. He can run all day like the wind and pull sleds and other things."

"If you've trained him to the harness, then you've done more than I could accomplish." He dismounted from his horse and walked with the others toward the trees where they did their cooking. A fire smouldered, keeping water close to the boil.

Peggy and Meg hurried across the yard toward them with Robbie running behind to keep up. "Monsieur Dauphin, it's nice to see you," Peggy said, shaking his hand warmly. "You catch us in the midst of our chores. We don't get visitors very often."

Dauphin smiled broadly and replied, "Ah, yes. It can be a lonely spot out here." Then he turned to Meg and said, "And here is the girl that I have heard so much about."

Meg blushed deeply. "And I've heard good things of you, sir."

Dauphin and the Bains family settled around the fire pit; Jamie added some buffalo chips to the coals, and the water heated to a boil as they talked. They spoke in French.

"You have finished your house I can see."

"Well, almost finished it," said Peggy. "We need windows, a door and a stove. But it will be nice and cosy once it is completed."

"So why have you not finished?"

"We'll have to go into town to buy the glass and door. The truth is, Monsieur Dauphin, we'll have to wait until the harvest comes in before we have the money."

"I can see that you're growing a good crop, and your garden is coming along nicely."

Peggy smiled. "Thanks to all of my children. I couldn't have done it without their help.

"Just hope that the grasshoppers don't come and eat it all."

Meg could not hold back any longer. "Monsieur Dauphin, have you heard from Louis?"

He smiled at her and asked, "Have you seen much of Campbell and the farmers?" It was clear that he needed some answers before he could trust them.

"Not for a while," replied Meg. "We seem to be unpopular with our neighbours."

He smiled sadly. "All the Métis people are unpopular with the English. Every few days Mr. Campbell and the others come down our way looking for Louis. I tell them he's gone, but they won't listen."

"But is Louis all right?" Meg asked.

"The prairie is wide and vast. It is hard to know."

"Meg is concerned," Peggy explained.

"He's a man on the run, thanks to your neighbours. Louis has to be careful, and those of us who know him have to be cautious, as well. But as it happens, a cart driver brought me a letter from him and inside was a letter addressed to ..." He pulled an envelope out of a sack he was carrying and carefully read the name on it. "Addressed to Meg Bains. I believe that is you," and he handed the letter to her with a smile.

Meg was completely taken by surprise. "A letter for me? Oh, *merci, Monsieur Dauphin. Merci beaucoup.*" She took the letter from his hand and studied the writing on the envelope for the longest time. Slowly she got to her feet and walked away from the others, holding the letter in her hand, examining every aspect of it. Then, in a rush, she tore open the envelope, took out the letter, and began reading it. A smile crept across Meg's face, and then she was beaming.

"Good news?" Peggy whispered to the Métis.

"How can a person our age judge a thing like that?" replied Dauphin, smiling.

Meg wandered off to be alone, and the others drank their tea and chatted. Peggy managed to turn the conversation to the issue that was nagging her. "Monsieur Dauphin, what do you do for the education of your children?"

"That is a problem, Madam Bains. I've been fighting for schooling for my children from the time that Louis was a baby."

"But what do you do now?"

"My wife and I have to teach the younger ones ourselves. Reading, writing, a little arithmetic, that is all we can give them. I am no teacher. Once the children are eleven or twelve, we send them off to the French mission school in St. Boniface. Louis went there. I went there myself many years ago."

Peggy leaned forward and said, "Well, I want to organize a school here in our community for my children and all the others. Would you send your younger children to a school like that?"

Dauphin was thoughtful for a moment. "An English school?" he asked.

Peggy nodded. "Yes."

"A Protestant school?"

"Yes, I imagine it would be run by Protestants, but it would be open to everyone regardless of what language they speak or what religion they have."

"I don't know, Madam Bains. The English don't like us Métis. Would the children get along?"

"They're going to have to get along. We are all going to live in this community for a long time."

"Well, I'll have to think about it. We're Métis people, not the same as you English."

Peggy smiled and said, "We're not so very different. We would have a teacher who could tell the children about geography, and music and grammar and literature and any number of wonderful things. It would be such a rich experience for them, don't you see? The Métis children could learn some English, and the English could learn some French."

"You make it sound wonderful, but I am not so sure."

"Maybe we can talk about it again."

Dauphin got to his feet and drained the rest of the tea he had in his cup. He moved beside his horse and scanned the horizon for a moment before turning back to the others. He seemed pensive and sad.

"This is the time of the year that the Métis gathered in Pembina for the buffalo hunt. I went every year from the time I was a small boy. The last years I was the captain of the hunt. Now the buffalo have gone. For two — three years they have disappeared. Vanished. Three buffalo hunters just returned from a scouting trip. They rode from here to the Badlands in the south, west as far as the Cypress Hills, and followed the northern tree line back home, but they found nothing. Not a buffalo anywhere."

"What will the Métis do?" Kate asked.

He swung into the saddle of his horse. "I don't know. It means there will be many hungry people — Métis and Indian alike."

Dauphin began to ride away toward the north. *"Au revoir,"* he said, waving his hat. Then he reined in his horse and turned back toward the camp as if he had thought of something special.

"My buffalo horses — are they still around?" he asked.

*"Oui,"* Jamie replied. "They're grazing a little to the west of here. I saw them yesterday."

"Choose another pony for yourself. It looks like I will not have need of them," he said, then wheeled his horse around and rode away.

The three younger Bains kids were overwhelmed by their good luck. In a rush they saddled up their pony and headed out to look for the horses. They found them some distance away grazing contentedly on prairie grass. Kate slid off the back of the pony, and the two boys followed.

The three of them inspected the herd, discussing the qualities they liked and disliked about the horses. The pony they finally selected was a brown mare that stood a little taller than the others. She was strong but still had that high-spirited look of all the ponies that had been used in the buffalo hunt.

Jamie had brought along a rope and got it around the pony's neck. They took off the hobble from the front legs and set off to lead her back to the farm.

"Let me ride on her back," Robbie said, and the others agreed it would help the horse get the feel of a rider.

Jamie boosted his brother onto the horse. "Hold on to her mane and grip her with your knees," he instructed.

"I know how to ride a horse," Robbie replied, annoyed that Jamie was telling him what to do.

The mare froze, her eyes wide. Suddenly, unexpectedly, she reared up on her hind legs. Robbie fought to keep aboard. Then she pitched forward, kicking her hind legs with all her strength. The wild pony began bucking and fighting to get rid of the rider. Robbie held on for dear life, digging his knees into the side of the horse, and gripping the mane with all of his strength. Jamie was holding onto the rope that was around the horse's neck. He pulled on it and found himself being dragged across the ground. Kate grabbed onto the rope, and the two of them were dragged around by the bucking horse.

But Robbie held to the horse's back like a burr lodged in fur. The pony bucked furiously, trying with every ounce of strength to dislodge the rider, but the boy would not be moved. Finally, as if realizing that the rider was not going to be thrown off her back, the horse stopped bucking and stood quivering and sweating from the effort.

"What a ride!" shouted Kate. "What a rider you are, Robbie!"

Jamie held the rope tight as he came to stroke the horse's neck and help calm her down. "It looks like you have earned this horse, Robbie," he said.

Once the mare had calmed, Kate and Jamie climbed back onto the buffalo pony and led the mare, with Robbie aboard, back to the farm. They did not mention the incident to their mother. She still thought of her youngest boy as a baby who needed protection. If she knew he had been riding a bucking bronco she would be horrified.

The next day, as the three of them were beginning to train their new horse, Dauphin appeared again. He was driving a cow before his horse, and he carried a sack tied to his saddle. Peggy met him near the fire pit.

Dauphin never got off his horse. "The cow, Madam Bains, is for the children. They need the milk to grow strong. And this ..." He reached into the sack and pulled out a chicken that flapped and squawked in an effort to get away. "This hen is for the rest of you. Every farm needs to have lots of chickens."

"Monsieur Dauphin, we can't accept this from you," Peggy said, shaking her head in disbelief.

"It is from your Métis neighbours, madam. We have learned in this wild country that we have to help one another if we are to survive."

"But you have been so generous. The horses and now this ..."

"It is no more than we would do for anyone else who has need."

"But how can we repay you?"

The Métis man held up his hand to say that he did not want to talk about it anymore. "Oh and one thing else." He reached into the sack and pulled out a bridle, which he threw on the ground toward Jamie. "For your new pony," he said. "We don't have another saddle, but you will find this helpful." Without another word he turned his horse and rode back the way he had come.

Peggy waved and called out, *"Merci, Monsieur Dauphin, merci ... merci."* She was so overwhelmed by the generosity that tears welled up in her eyes. It was like the Dauphins and the Métis were family to them. They saw that the Bainses were in need, and they gave what they could afford. Generosity was part of the way they lived their lives.

The family sat around the fire pit to talk about their good fortune. "I want you always to remember how people have helped us," said their mother. "Never forget that."

"But where are we going to keep the cow?" asked Meg.

"She can range just like the horses," replied Jamie.

"You'd better tether her," said Peggy. "The animals are going to get into the garden and ruin the plants. I noticed that your buffalo pony got into a part of the wheat field the other day. We have to build some sort of a pen for them."

This sparked a long family discussion. Finally they agreed that they would build a corral to hold the livestock and cut hay for the animals to eat over the winter. A stable for the cow and Baby was needed to help them get through the winter, and they would build a hen house. It was a lot of work, but everyone agreed that those things were necessary.

After lunch Jamie headed off toward the river with the buffalo pony pulling the sled. He carried the axe and spent the afternoon cutting and hauling trees. When he returned, he had at least two dozen long poles tied onto the sled. Jamie took several trips down to the trees along the river bank, and each time he returned with stacks of poles for the big building project.

In the meantime Kate and Robbie were training their new horse. Jamie fitted the bridle before he went away. Robbie climbed up onto the horse's back, half expecting that she would attempt to buck him off again, but she was calm this time as if she had learned her lesson from the last ride. Kate led the mare around the yard, letting her get the feel of a rider on her back.

Not having a saddle made it more difficult to ride. Robbie could grasp onto the horse's back with his knees, but without the stirrups it was difficult to move with the rhythm of the horse.

After they had been walking around for a time, with Kate leading, Robbie persuaded his sister to let him ride by himself. Once he had gathered the reins, and Kate moved out of the way, the horse stood completely still until Robbie poked her with his heels. Slowly she began walking. Robbie nudged her again. Immediately the horse responded by trotting, and then with another kick she went faster. Robbie found that he could make her respond to his every command. "This is going to be easy," he told Kate. "The horse must have been ridden before."

But it wasn't so easy. They worked for hours to train the animal. They each took turns riding so that the mare could get the feel of different riders. They took her up to a gallop and steered through manoeuvres. After a couple of days of training, Jamie took a barebacked ride on the new horse himself. He was amazed at how well the animal responded.

But there was still lots of work. It became Kate and Robbie's chore to milk the cow at dawn and sundown. She was a stubborn beast who would try to move away or kick over the pail. They had to milk her while she was tethered with a rope staked to the ground. The cow moved around while they chased her. Finally, the only thing they could do was to have one of them stand on one side of the cow, holding her, while the other stayed on the other side and did the milking.

There were benefits. The warm, frothy milk was delicious, and they could drink as much as they wanted. Everyone loved the milk on porridge in the morning, and mugs of it were drunk at every meal.

After Jamie had gathered enough of the poles, the family pitched in to build the corral. They had no nails so they built it like the cedar snake fences that Peggy remembered on

Ottawa Valley farms. At the ends, each pole was stacked on top of another until the poles were high enough to keep the animals inside.

The day they finished the corral, Albert suddenly appeared, riding on his big workhorse. He was alone, but he carried his rifle in the long holster on the saddle.

"I can see you're developin' quite a spread here," he said with an edge to his voice. "Is it your hard work, or is it that you're still real friendly with them Métis?" His clean-shaven face showed his simmering anger.

Peggy was dressed in her rough men's clothes she had brought to work in. "We work for ourselves, and we're beholden to no one."

"Our friends are our business," added Meg in an unfriendly tone.

"Just in case you didn't know, there is a reward for the capture of Louis Dauphin," he laughed. "Might be a way of makin' a little money."

Meg was furious. "That warrant is a total lie, Albert!" she shouted. "Totally untrue and you know it!"

"What about you, boy? Want to make a little money?"

"You leave him out of this!" ordered Peggy, angrily.

Albert laughed. "Just thought I'd ride by and tell you the news about the reward. And by the way, if you see Louis, you be sure to let us know. You don't want to break the law by protectin' a wanted criminal." He kicked his horse and rode off in the direction of the Dauphins' place.

"I hate that man!" said Meg under her breath.

"As long as Louis stays away, there will be no trouble," replied Peggy. "Let's get back to work."

The next day they finished the corral and began work on a sod stable large enough for the cow and Baby. Beside it was a little chicken coop, but they did not have a chicken to live in it. The hen that Dauphin had brought them ran around the yard for days. Often they would find eggs in a grass nest or in a pile of hay, but one day the hen disappeared. Jamie was sure the badger that he often saw had got her, but no one knew for sure.

Early one morning Jamie and Kate met the young Indian boy and went hunting in the meadows down by the trees that lined the river. Even though they could not speak the same language, the Indian taught them how to stay upwind and creep in close to their quarry. He dropped a young buck with one shot from his Winchester rifle.

Kate was upset when she saw the deer up close.

"Remember what Louis said," Jamie reminded her. "We have to learn to live off the land, like the Indians and Métis, or we will never survive."

The venison was shared between the hunters and for the first time in months the Bains family was able to eat its fill of fresh meat.

The family spent more and more time cutting hay to store for the winter. All they had was a little hand sickle to cut the long prairie grass. One of them would cut while the others piled the grass into the Red River cart. Once they had a big enough load, Baby would haul it over to the growing pile of hay near the stable.

With the monotony of the work, one day seemed to merge into the next. Often Meg would be seen scanning the horizon. Peggy worried about the ever decreasing supplies of basics such as flour and oatmeal. Jamie, Kate, and Robbie kept busy with unending chores of milking, haying, cutting wood, and training the horses.

The wheat grew tall and toward the end of August began to turn a yellowish colour. The vegetable garden began to ripen, and the diet of the Bains family improved with small potatoes and carrots.

One day they realized that the number of grasshoppers had increased. The next day there were even more. Peggy feared that they would be overrun with the insects. She had heard stories about how grasshoppers had wiped out an entire crop by eating everything in the farm in a matter of hours. It became her worst fear. But then, miraculously, birds came and began eating the hoppers. They arrived in the thousands, and the grasshoppers disappeared.

It was a hot, dry day in late August. The family was in the western section of the farm cutting hay when Meg looked up and saw a horseman riding toward them a long way in the distance. She stopped what she was doing and watched the horseman approach. The others stopped working and waited.

The horseman was riding in an easy canter. He wore a big-brimmed hat to protect him from the sun and the weather. From a distance it was hard to see the rider, but the horse was a familiar stallion. The man wore a tan pull-over shirt with a red sash around his waist. Then they could see it was Louis.

Meg ran through the grass toward him. "Louis! … Louis!" she called excitedly. The Métis man was laughing. He leaned down and easily swept her up in his arms and placed her in front of him on his horse.

# 15

Louis had grown even more handsome since he had been away. His face was thinner, and his skin had darkened from the hours on the trail. His long black hair was gathered in a leather thong at the back of his head. He looked lean and fit, with a more mature confidence in himself.

"Where have you been, Louis?" Kate asked excitedly.

"West," was his only reply.

Peggy laughed and said, "I can say for everyone here, it's nice to have you back."

"I have been away too long." He was speaking English. "But I have news of many things."

"Stay for tea, and we can talk."

"No. I must see my family. I have much news to tell my father."

"But you must talk with me before you go anywhere else," Meg said, overcome with the excitement and joy of the moment. She looked happier than at any time since Louis had gone away.

He laughed and replied, "That is an invitation I cannot pass upon."

Meg slipped off his horse and Louis climbed down to the ground. The two were oblivious to the others. They walked, hand in hand, out onto the prairie, whispering. Periodically one or the other could be heard laughing as they shared a secret.

"I think something's going to happen between them," Kate whispered to Jamie, then giggled.

"I thought Mother said you shouldn't talk like that," he said, looking very earnest and grown up.

"Don't be an old stick-in-the-mud, Jamie. You're as interested as I am."

The boy looked at his sister and then laughed. He knew she was right.

Meg and Louis were not away for long. As they approached the others, they stopped holding hands, trying to hide the obvious affection they shared.

"I must go," Louis said, swinging into the saddle. *"Au revoir,"* and without another word he rode off toward the trees that lined the Assiniboine.

"Well, Meg, did he kiss you?" Kate asked, smirking.

But Meg paid absolutely no attention to her younger sister. She was too wrapped up in the exquisite feelings of the moment. Louis had returned, and that was all she could think of. He had returned and now everything was possible.

That night, after they finished work, Meg bathed in the stream and put on her good frock. She was too excited to talk to the family. She sat near the fire with the others, combing out her long hair, preoccupied with her own thoughts.

"Do you smell that?" asked Jamie

"What?" said Peggy.

"Smoke."

All of the others stopped and looked up. There was a haze in the air. In the west the sun was setting in one of the most spectacular displays that they had seen since they had arrived on the prairie.

Peggy walked away from the campsite so she could get a better sense of the air. "Yes," she said finally. "There is definitely the smell of smoke."

"What do you think it's from?" Jamie asked. He had come to stand beside his mother.

"I don't know. Maybe a settler's burning off some grass. Or maybe there's a forest fire up north."

"Maybe ..." repeated Jamie. "Or maybe there is a grass fire a long way out on the prairie."

"Don't frighten us like that," Peggy said and turned back toward her cooking.

But the smell of smoke would not go away. Louis returned after supper to walk out with Meg. Jamie asked him about the smoke. The Métis stood for a long time, looking to the south and the west.

"It's a grass fire somewhere out on the prairie," he announced. "She's a long way away, and it could be travelling in any direction. Depends on the direction of the wind."

As Meg and Louis walked out onto the prairie, a full moon rose, casting a pale, beautiful light across the barren landscape. Owls hooted in the darkness, and bats flew around catching insects, but the couple was unaware of anything but themselves.

It was late at night, and everyone was asleep except Peggy, when Meg returned. The mother smiled at her daughter, put away her darning and got ready for bed. She said nothing. They would have lots of time to talk when decisions had been made and things were more settled.

Every morning for weeks Peggy had risen early and visited the fields. The sun shone out of a hazy but clear sky. The wheat, swaying in the southern breeze, had ripened into a golden colour. The kernels of grain were swelling. In a week they would begin the harvest.

She felt a quickening excitement. The family was out of money, but with the wheat crop harvested its future would be secured. With a little money, they could afford to buy a stove, windows, and a door for the house. They would have food for winter, and maybe even a few luxuries.

How long had it been since they had bought new clothes for themselves? Maybe with a little extra money they could buy beds and bedding. Chocolates and sweets were almost forgotten by the children. Perhaps, if there was enough money, they could buy lumber and build a real house.

Peggy smiled to herself. Something was about to happen with Meg. She knew it. If they had just a little bit of money, the family would be able to provide her with something so she could start a new life with some security. No one deserved that more than Meg. It would make her the happiest mother in the world if she could provide this for her daughter.

Yet there was still that smell of smoke. It was stronger now. She searched the horizon and saw what looked like the trace of black clouds to the south. Could a grass fire spread and travel all the way north to their homestead? She just did not know.

Peggy turned away and walked toward the vegetable garden. There was so much to worry about: grasshoppers, hail, fire. What if the crop was destroyed? She shuddered to think of it. Everything depended on this harvest.

After breakfast the members of the family went back out into the field to cut hay. They were sweating under the hot sun when one of them spotted the three farmers approaching on their big horses.

"Morning," said Mr. Campbell as they rode up. Jamie noticed that this time all three of them carried weapons.

Peggy spoke for the family. "Morning, gentlemen. It's been a long time since you've been out this way."

"That's the truth," replied Campbell.

Then Albert added, "Maybe if we had been made to feel more welcome then we surely would have been here more often." He glanced at Meg as if to underline his point.

"Friendliness is a thing that we value, Albert. I just wish that others would value our neighbours as much as we do."

"That's them Métis that yer talkin' about." Anger was in his voice. "We know all about your love of them."

"Settle down, Albert. We're here on business," said Campbell, trying to take control of the conversation. "Louis Dauphin has been seen in the neighbourhood. There's still a warrant out for his arrest and now there's a reward. Do you know where he is?"

"Back in the neighbourhood, is he?" replied Peggy for the family. "Can't say that I know where he is right now."

"Can't say or just won't say?" asked Albert aggressively.

"Hold yer tongue!" said Frank, who looked increasingly uncomfortable.

"They're coverin' up for him. These Bainses are in with the Métis thick as thieves."

"Are you calling us thieves, sir?" Peggy demanded.

"Take it any way you want!"

"Albert, if you carry this on, I'm leavin' right now," warned Frank. "I won't have women talked to like this!"

"You'll see that I'm proven right in the end." Albert kicked his horse, and his big animal began trotting in the direction of the river and the Dauphin place.

"Sorry, ma'am," said Frank, but he followed Albert, and Campbell trailed behind.

"I don't like the looks of this," Peggy said, as they rode away.

"If I got the buffalo pony, I might be able to get to the Dauphins before them and warn Louis," said Jamie.

"Louis can look after himself," was her only comment.

As they worked the rest of the morning they watched for the return of the farmers but saw no one. That did not mean anything. There was a trail along the river, in among the trees that they could take back to Campbell's place and not be seen.

Meg was worried. Albert might resort to violence for any reason at all. Why was he so angry at Louis and the Métis?

Could it be that he hated them simply because they were French and Catholic?

Jamie wanted to go down to the Dauphins' to find out what had happened, but his mother refused to let him. The boy was only fourteen, after all, and there was altogether too much unpredictable anger in this situation.

It was early in the afternoon when Robbie looked up from his work and pointed to the south. "Look!"

Black smoke lined the horizon. The grass fire appeared to be bigger now.

"What can we do?" Jamie asked.

Peggy studied the sky. "I don't know. Grass fires can wipe out a whole farm in a matter of minutes. If it comes this way then …"

The boy stood looking across the prairie at the rising smoke. The last rainfall had been about three weeks before. The grass was yellow and tinder-dry. The wheat grew right up to the edge of the field and merged with the grass. If the fire swept down on them, how could they save their crops? Even their sod house, corral, and stable could go up in flames. They had only three pails they could fill with water. Was that enough to stop a raging grass fire?

"Come on Kate," Jamie said.

Their two ponies were grazing a few yards away. Jamie got the buffalo pony, and Kate climbed onto the mare. The two rode out to the wheat field.

At the south side of the field, they reined in. The breeze had picked up and was blowing toward them from the south. The black smoke now covered the entire southern horizon, it billowed upward, towering hundreds of feet in the sky. The air was alive with insects and birds fleeing from the fire. Now Jamie was convinced that the fire was sweeping down on them.

"Someone's coming!" Kate pointed south, toward the fire.

A horseman was approaching at a full gallop. He had his hat off and was using it to hit the flanks of his animal.

"It's Louis," Kate said. They got on their horses and rode in the direction of the racing horseman. When Louis saw them, he rode up and reined his horse in at the very last moment. His horse was in a heavy lather. He had been running for a long time.

"Grass fire!" Louis shouted. "It's coming fast! We have to warn the others!"

Without another word, Louis spurred his mount and rode toward the sod hut. Jamie and Kate followed him as best they could. Peggy, Meg, and Robbie met them at the entrance way to the house. Louis did not bother to dismount.

"The wind is up behind the fire, and driving it this way," the young Métis explained, panting as hard as his horse. "I rode out this morning to take a look. It's a huge fire, maybe twenty miles wide, and it's coming this way at a terrible rate."

"The wheat field!" cried Peggy. "What do we do?"

"I'm riding for my father and the others. I'll be back!"

But just at that moment, they looked up to see the three farmers riding toward them. They had been hiding in the brush along by the creek bed. All three had their weapons out, and they were pointed at Louis.

"You're not goin' nowhere," said Albert.

"What?"

"I thought we'd find you here. The Bains family has been hidin' you out, haven't they?"

"No one hid me!"

"This time you're not gettin' away Louis." Albert's voice had a threatening edge. "Now, get down off that horse."

"The fire's coming. Don't you see? I've got to warn the others," Louis shouted.

"You're not going to scare us. Get off your horse!" Albert moved his gun up to take aim.

"Look!" Louis exclaimed, pointing to the southern horizon. The black smoke filled the sky. "Our only chance is to fight it now!"

"You're not going to use that trick to escape this time. Now, get off your horse before my finger slips on the trigger!" Albert's anger made him frightening.

Louis looked from Albert to Meg and back to Albert again. Slowly he got off his horse without another word. Meg ran up to him, crying.

"Well, isn't this just the nice family picture," Albert said scornfully.

Jamie stepped forward. "You leave my sister alone!" he warned, pointing at Albert threateningly. "If anything happens to her, I'll get you for it."

"Now, now, let's not lose our heads," Campbell said, trying to defuse the tension.

"If anyone has lost his head, Campbell, it's you," shouted Peggy angrily. "We're going to fight this to the end. It's nothing but a bunch of trumped-up charges!"

"The court issued the warrant!"

"You made this happen, Campbell! I hold you responsible!"

"Give me your hands," ordered Albert. "You're going to be tied up like a chicken ready for roasting."

Curiously Louis complied without a struggle. "Fools," he said softly, in his French accent. "Fools who face disaster and still fiddle with things of no importance."

Albert tied his wrists together tightly. "You should count yourself lucky that we caught you peaceful, like. Otherwise we might not have to take you in at all. Now get on your horse."

"I'm going with you," Meg announced suddenly.

"What do you mean?" asked Albert, confused.

"You heard me. I'm going with you. I don't trust you, Albert. You're a bad man, and you just might find the opportunity to do something terrible to Louis."

"You can't come!"

"You don't think so! Try and stop me." She stood, hands on hips, an angry, defiant look on her face.

"I won't allow it!"

"Leave her be, for God's sake," said Frank. "Let her come if she wants to."

Albert could do nothing in the face of the opposition. They mounted Louis up on his own horse and tied the rope that bound his wrists onto the saddle. Meg climbed up behind him on the horse. Frank took the reins and led the prisoner away.

As they were riding out of the yard, Louis called back in French. "*Cherchez mon père*. Forget about me. Fight the fire. It is for your survival!"

# 16

For a moment the family seemed paralyzed. There was so much to do and so little time to do it. Then Jamie sprang into action.

"Kate, ride to the Dauphins' place. Tell them what happened. Say that we need their help to save the farm. The fire's coming!"

Without a word Kate ran for the mare and scrambled on top of her. She pulled her long skirt around her, clutched onto the bare back of the pony with her knees, and gave a boot with her heels. The horse thundered out of the yard toward the river and the Dauphin place with the girl crouched over her back.

It was as if the mare understood the urgency. Kate whispered into her ear. "Faster, pony, faster!" and the horse galloped with a speed that she had never felt before. They raced across the open prairie, the animal's hooves pounding on the hard-packed earth, eating up the ground with every stride.

They raced along the trail by the creek and past the marsh. Once they were into the trees, the land fell away quickly, and Kate had to rein in the horse until they found the wagon road. Again she shouted some indistinguishable command, and the horse leapt into a gallop again. The trees whipped by them in a flash, and in minutes the horse and rider broke into the clearing of the farm.

"Dauphin! Dauphin!" she shouted as they sped toward the log house.

The Métis man came out of the stable. He was startled by Kate's urgency. "What's wrong?" he asked in French.

"The fire's sweeping down on our farm. Louis has been arrested by Campbell and the farmers. You must help!"

Madame Dauphin and the children had come out of the house sensing the panic. Dauphin grasped the halter of Kate's horse and tried to calm them both. "The fire? Louis? What do you mean?"

Kate explained as calmly as possible. It did not take long for Dauphin to understand the situation. Quickly he issued a series of orders.

"Joseph," he called to a son about the same age as Kate. "Take your pony and ride to the Métis along the river! Warn them about the fire and say we need every man who can be spared to help the Bains family. We'll meet at their farm!"

Before he had even finished, the boy ran like the wind to the corral where they kept their ponies. In a moment he was on the back of a horse and was riding along the wagon road to the east.

"Mother, I'll put the two rain barrels into the cart and put the ox to the yoke," Dauphin continued. "You bring the other children and the cart. We'll fill the barrels in the creek!"

"What about Louis?" Kate asked.

"We'll think about him later. For now the fire is the thing."

It seemed that everyone ran in every direction, but it took almost no time to get organized. Madame Dauphin headed out driving the ox with the cart, which contained the two rain barrels and three young children. Kate and Dauphin rode ahead on their horses, racing back as fast as they could to the Bainses' homestead.

At the farm Jamie, Robbie, and their mother had hurried to the south side of the wheat field as soon as Kate had ridden in search of help. For a moment they stood in awe, watching the approaching fire. The black smoke covered the entire southern horizon. Now they could see the angry red flames leaping into the sky. How far away was the fire? It was hard to know, but the south wind was up, and it was driving the flames toward them at a furious rate.

Jamie looked around desperately. There had to be something that they could do to protect the wheat field and the farm. But what? The flames would sweep down on them, driven by a wind created by the fire itself; flaming grass would leap before the wall of flames, starting new fires that would be impossible to put out. It would sweep through the dry wheat field in less than a minute.

"We should have ploughed a firebreak," Jamie said, panting.

"It's too late now," replied their mother.

They needed some kind of a barrier of open ground several paces wide that would not burn — but how could they create one? The boy tried to think. They could hear the roar of the fire in the distance. How could they stop this fire storm? They had to try!

"We can burn a backfire, mother," Jamie shouted.

"What?"

"We need a swath of barren land between the wheat field and the approaching fire to act as a firebreak. The only thing we can do is to burn the grass now while we can control it. We'll fight fire with fire!"

"How do we do that?" Robbie asked.

"Listen carefully. We have no time to loose!"

Jamie issued orders as quickly as possible. Robbie ran for the matches in the hut. Their mother brought all the old burlap seed bags that they owned. Jamie went to the creek with their three pails, filled them with water, and struggled back to the south side of the wheat field.

Three pails of water. That wasn't nearly enough, he thought. How could they fight a raging grass fire and save their farm with three pails of water, some matches, and burlap bags? But they must try.

When they were ready, Jamie, Peggy, and Robbie lit torches of dried grass and went out twenty paces or more beyond the wheat field to set the prairie grass on fire. It was tinder-dry and began burning immediately. The wind caught it and spread the fire quickly. The three of them watched as the flames burned toward the wheat. The thick smoke caught in their noses and throats and made the burned grass charcoal black in an instant.

Closer and closer the fire burned toward the wheat. The three of them waited, soaking wet burlap bags in their hands; the fire came nearer, crackling through the dry grass as it burned. Could they control their own fire, or would it reduce everything in its path to cinders?

"Now!" Jamie said and the three of them began to beat out the flames. They flailed at their fire with wet burlap bags for what seemed like the longest time. Robbie was having trouble. Jamie ran to help him once he had his patch under control. In a moment the fire was out, and all that was left was the smouldering blackened earth.

They had burned a patch of ground, but it only protected a small part of the wheat field. They would have to do far more before they would have a swath of ground large enough to protect the farm.

They moved down the field and started again. First they set the torches alight and started a line of fires twenty paces away from the wheat. They waited. Again the fire crept through the grass, burning all the years of accumulated dried dead grass as it inched along toward the wheat. They waited until the very last moment and then with a cry from Jamie, they began beating at the flames with their burlap bags.

In one spot the flames got out of control and spread into the field. Jamie plunged through the waist-high wheat. The flames were growing rapidly. He pounded at them with his burlap bag. Over and over again he flailed away until he could feel a stabbing pain from the effort spreading through his shoulders and down his back. But he would not stop, he had to get every last bit of fire out.

"Jamie! Jamie!" his mother called in panic.

The boy raced back. The fire flared up even higher. Robbie and their mother were beating at it, but it was almost out of control. Jamie plunged into the flames, beating away furiously. Pounding, pounding, pounding. They had to get the fire out or else they would be consumed themselves. The boy's pant legs were on fire. He felt a quick searing pain before he beat it out with his burlap bag.

Finally, finally it was out. They slumped on the ground with exhaustion. Jamie looked up. The smoke from the grass fire was a huge pall that now covered the entire sky. He could see the red angry flames and hear the deafening roar. Their firebreak protected less than half of the wheat field. There was no time for rest.

Again they lit the torches. Again they set fire to the grass twenty paces out from the wheat field. Again it burned down upon the wheat. And again they began to pound away at the fire with their wet burlap bags as it got to the very edge of the wheat field.

This time the fire they set was even more out of control. The water was finished, and they flailed away at the flames with the bags barely damp. But no one was going to give up. Robbie was nearing exhaustion. The strength needed to pound at the blaze was almost too much for him, but the young boy would not give up. The three of them beat the flames with every bit of strength and energy that they could muster and finally they were able to stamp them out.

"I'm going to get some more water," Jamie shouted. "Robbie, get the buffalo pony and hitch the harrow to it. We're going to defeat this fire yet!"

"The harrow? What for?"

"Just get it and hurry!"

The two boys took off in a run, leaving their mother guarding the wheat field. Jamie struggled back with the three overfilled pails of water just as Robbie came with the horse dragging their wooden makeshift harrow.

"I don't understand why you want this," Robbie yelled.

"You'll see."

Again they set their backfire. This time they were able to bring it under control much better because their burlap bags were soaked with water. They were almost finished burning the break for the wheat field.

"Robbie, do you think you can control the horse and the harrow by yourself?" Jamie asked.

"I think so."

"What you're going to do is harrow this burned section. We're going to scrape this firebreak of ours down to bare earth. There won't be anything left for that grass fire to burn. Do you think you can do it yourself?"

"I don't know, but I can try."

It took all of Robbie's strength and concentration. The buffalo pony could see the fire coming as well, and it made him extremely skittish. The young boy had to control the horse at the same time as he controlled their wooden harrow. Twice the pony started to bolt, but Robbie would not let go of the reins. He dug his heels into the ground and dragged along until the horse stopped.

"Easy, boy, easy. We're going to be just fine," he said, talking to the high-spirited horse continually in an attempt to ease his fear of the approaching fire.

The horse has to have confidence in the driver. That's what Jamie had taught. He has to listen to your voice and feel that you know what you are doing.

"The fire won't touch us," Robbie repeated over and over again. I'll look after you, pony. Just pull the harrow nice and easy. We'll be fine."

The eyes of the buffalo pony were frightened, but the familiar voice and the confidence of Robbie seemed to give him reassurance that everything was going to be all right. They began again, and this time the horse responded. He walked along at a good pace, still frightened, but firmly under control.

Robbie guided the horse with the reins and manoeuvred the harrow at the same time so that the wooden stakes attached to the bottom scratched at the burned grass and dragged away the surface debris leaving bare, charred earth. There would be nothing for the approaching grass fire to burn.

Peggy and Jamie were burning another section of the firebreak when Dauphin galloped up. Immediately the Métis man jumped off his horse and helped them beat out the flames. Kate rode up and joined them. It took minutes but finally all of the flames were out.

They paused for a moment for a rest without saying a word. The fire was closing in upon them. They could clearly see the wall of angry red and yellow flames. It was still some distance away, but it was closing in on them fast.

"She's a big one," Dauphin said in French. "Biggest grass fire I've seen for many years."

"Can we defeat it?" Jamie asked.

"Problem with fires this big is that firebrands are thrown up high into the air and are blown behind you. They can be blown sometimes half a mile or more. We have to chase each one of them down and beat them out."

"How do we do that?"

"We'll need every hand that we can muster." Dauphin looked around for a moment to assess the situation. "Your firebreak is great, Jamie. Brilliant, and using that harrow to scrape the ground is even better."

"We're going to have to extend it," the boy explained. "It will have to go down along the garden so it can protect the house and the garden."

"It's a long way. We'll try. But we need every hand."

Dauphin stood looking across at the fire. They could hear the roar of the wind and the flames. The sound was terrifying.

Suddenly Dauphin turned to the boy. "Jamie, you will have to go and get Louis and Meg."

"Louis? But he's under arrest."

"That's all a pack of foolishness. We need every experienced man we can get. Our survival depends on defeating this fire. Go and get him now!"

"But they won't listen to me!"

"I would go myself except I speak no English. We need them both, and we need them now. Go!"

Jamie stood for a moment and then ran for the brown mare. He vaulted onto her bare back and raced as fast as the horse would take him toward Campbell's place.

# 17

Jamie raced along the worn path, west toward the Campbell farm. The mare was tired from the hard ride that Kate had taken down to the Dauphin place, but she seemed to sense the urgency and galloped with all the strength in her lean body.

Every moment or so Jamie would look toward the approaching fire. The black smoke now covered the entire southern sky, billowing up in great clouds as the blaze raced over the grasslands, consuming everything in its path. The boy could see red flames across the entire front of the inferno.

If only he could release Louis and Meg and get back in time to help save the farm. That one thought was like a fire inside him consuming all of his energy, taking all of his concentration. They had to save the farm. The family's future depended upon it.

Ahead of him Jamie saw a deer bounding across the path north, toward the river. A prairie chicken was half running, half flying in the same direction. The badger, who he was sure had stolen their chicken, darted right in front of the sharp hooves of the horse and kept on going, oblivious to everything.

Every wild animal was on the move, trying to flee from the approaching conflagration: small gophers were scurrying, snakes slithered, birds of every species and description flew upward. All of them were heading north as fast as they could travel. They knew instinctively that they had to get out of the way of the fire or die in the flames.

Jamie and the horse raced west toward the Campbell place; the only living things on the prairie that were not moving out of the way of the approaching blaze. They thundered on until finally they arrived at the farm with its wood frame house standing alone on the prairie.

"Meg! Louis!" Jamie was shouting as he neared the house.

Meg ran out to meet him. Louis was sitting on the back of a wagon, tied to it at the wrists. Campbell and the two young farmers came hurrying out of the yard toward him.

"Fire!" Jamie shouted and pointed to the south. "Grass fire! We need every hand to help, or it will destroy us all!"

It was as if this was the first time that Campbell and the others took the fire seriously. All of them, Meg included, stood watching it, trying to comprehend the impending doom that it spelled.

"We need Louis and Meg!" Jamie yelled, trying to bring them back to reality. He climbed off his horse and moved toward the wagon where Louis was tied.

"What do you mean?" Campbell demanded.

"We need them back at our place to fight the fire!"

"You want to release Louis?"

"Yes!"

"But he's under arrest. There is the warrant —"

"We have to save ourselves, Campbell! Don't you understand?" Jamie was at the wagon now. He reached down to undo the ropes that bound Louis.

"You're not going to release that man!" said Albert in a low, threatening voice.

Jamie looked up. Albert had his rifle in his hands. He looked determined and dangerous. "We need him to fight this fire!" Jamie said with a calm, steady voice, but inside he could feel his stomach tighten.

"He's our prisoner!"

"You're a fool, Albert!" Jamie shot back.

The young farmer moved his rifle until the barrel was pointing at the boy. "We're gonna take him in and nobody's gonna stop us!"

"You should be thinking of saving yourself," Jamie said, then turned to Campbell and Frank. "All your farms will burn while you try to fight some invented threat by the Métis!"

Both Frank and Campbell turned and looked again at the raging fire. "I think he's right," said Campbell uncertainly.

Albert was in a fury now. "We've got a warrant!"

"You're crazy, Albert, crazy!" Jamie was yelling at him out of anger and fear and complete disbelief that he would be so foolish.

The farmer looked to Frank and then to Campbell. "They're rotten to the core, those Métis."

"But Albert …" Campbell seemed confused.

"I'm releasing him!" Jamie said, and he turned back to undo the knot that bound Louis' hands.

"Stand back, boy!"

"Albert! Put that gun down now!" Campbell suddenly ordered.

"But he's a criminal!"

"You heard me! Put that gun down! The boy's right! There's a fire comin'!"

"No, Campbell! We've got the warrant!"

"We've got to save our farms! We're going to let him go!"

Jamie glanced back in time to see Albert look desperately from Frank to Campbell. Slowly he dropped his gun. He had lost whatever support he needed to stop Jamie. The young farmer was humbled and subdued.

There was no time to think about it now. In a moment the prisoner was released, and Jamie, Louis, and Meg were running for their ponies.

The farmers were moving as well. Frank was shouting. "Albert, our farms. Got to save the crops — the animals." The two of them were aboard their big workhorses and in a moment were heading out toward their farms.

Campbell was yelling as he ran toward the house. "Ruby! Ruby! Fire! Get out the pails! We need water! Lots of it!"

But Jamie, Meg, and Louis did not hear another word. They were aboard their ponies heading back toward the Bainses' farm. Meg and Louis were out in front galloping as hard as the Métis' horse could take them. Jamie came behind. His pony was almost played out now, but the mare galloped as fast as she could toward the farm and toward the ever closer, raging grass fire.

The heat from the approaching fire was intense. As he raced in the direction of the farm, Jamie could see that the wall of flames was two or three hundred paces away and approaching at a steady speed. Brands of flaming grass were flying high into the air and were being blown ahead of the flames.

As the boy thundered into the yard, he could see maybe a dozen men and women standing in a line along the south side of the wheat field and the garden in the swath of land that they had burned. They were Métis people. Dauphin had organized them into an army to fight this enemy. There were barrels of water along the firebreak they had created on the perimeter of the farm. Each person had a soaking wet burlap bag in his hands. They were waiting for the attack, ready to pounce on any burning brands that might fall behind their lines.

Louis and Meg had dismounted and ran to positions near the vegetable garden. Robbie was up on the roof of the stable. Kate and the Dauphin boy, Joseph, were on the roof of the sod hut. All of them had wet burlap in their hands, and all of them were waiting for the oncoming enemy.

Jamie put his horse in the corral with the others and ran toward Dauphin, who was standing in the firebreak on the

south side of the wheat field. Without a word he took a burlap
sack, soaked it, and stood with the others. As he got ready he
glanced up and saw that it was his mother beside him. For just
a fraction of a second, she smiled at him and then looked back
at the approaching enemy.

The fire was no more than a hundred paces away. It
roared so loud that nothing else could be heard. The black and
white smoke swept down upon them, stinging their eyes and
catching in their lungs. The heat was unbearable, and as the
fire got closer it became more and more intense.

Firebrands were flying up all around them. One soared
over Jamie's head and into the wheat field. The boy raced
through the wheat to the spot and pounded at the ground with
his burlap bag until it was out. Another landed close by.
Again he flailed at the ground. Then another and another.
They were all around him. He flailed away at the burning
wheat, putting each flame out before it had the chance to
spread.

Once he looked up and saw that his mother was pounding
with her bag at the fires. The Métis beside them were doing
the same. All of them were fighting these flames with every
ounce of strength and endurance that they could muster.

Jamie raced back to the barrel of water and soaked his
bag again. As he glanced up, he could see that the fire had
burned right to the edge of the firebreak. There it seemed to
hesitate but continued to burn violently.

But the boy had no time to watch. Firebrands were continuing to fly over the firebreak and into the wheat field. He
plunged back into the field. A score of fires was blazing all
around them. He pounded at the fires until the wet burlap put
them out.

Someone was shouting. In the centre of the field a brand
had started a blaze that had burned a circle several paces in
diameter. Jamie plunged through the wheat to get to the fire.

Peggy and another man were there. Together they beat at the flames.

Suddenly there was a shout. "Jamie! Jamie!" It was his mother. He could see that her long skirt was on fire. He ran to her and flailed at the skirt with the wet burlap bag.

"Get it out! It's burning!" she cried in terror.

The boy tore at the material, smothering it with his bare hands. In the panic he couldn't think. He couldn't speak. All that he knew was that he had to extinguish the flames. Finally the skirt was smouldering. His mother was safe and unhurt.

Jamie ran back to get more water. Already the grass fire on the outside of the firebreak was beginning to die out as it burned the grass down to its roots. The scorched swath of land that they had burned as a firebreak had stopped the fire. On either side of the farm, the fire continued its onward advance to the north, but this pocket of the Bainses' farm had been saved.

Jamie ran back into the wheat field searching for more spots that might be burning but there were none. Patches of the wheat had been burned, even more had been trampled down by the firefighters, but the field had been saved.

As he searched for more fire, he met his mother doing the same. She was blackened almost beyond recognition. Her skirt had large burn holes, and her face was streaked from water flying off the burlap.

"Jamie, Jamie, we saved it." She was crying. "Our neighbours helped us save our farm." Big tears created white rivulets on her charcoal-blackened face. She collapsed into his arms sobbing, asking, "How can we ever thank them?"

The boy spoke softly to his mother, trying his best to comfort her, and then led her from the wheat field. She was exhausted, but the battle had been won. The fire had been defeated. The farm had been saved.

It was as Jamie was helping his mother that people gathered around. Dauphin was there with his wife and young children along with other Métis. The young Indian boy that they had met recently was there with them, as blackened as the others. He had seen the danger and had come to help. People were laughing, even cheering the victory. Meg and Louis ran up, and then Kate and Robbie. Peggy hugged them all, thanking them over and over again until they became embarrassed.

Louis had been standing outside the group, looking to the west. He turned and pointed. "Look! The fire has not reached the Campbell farm. Maybe we can save it." He spoke in French so that everyone could understand

"Do you think we can arrive in time?" someone asked.

"We can try. Everyone with a horse! Let's go!"

The horses had been held in the corral. Louis led the way, and the others followed. In a moment seven horses were mounted and riding out. Jamie was on top of the buffalo pony and Kate rode bareback on the mare. Joseph was there along with the Indian boy and a group of Métis men.

As they were going out the corral gate, Jamie heard a shout. It was Robbie waving his hands frantically. Jamie paused barely a moment to scoop his brother up and place him on the pony behind him.

Peggy was calling after them. "He's too young, Jamie."

Meg put her arm around her mother's shoulders. "He'll not be held back any more, Mother."

There was a break in the line of the fire where it had been stopped by the firebreak for the Bainses' farm. Louis led the way through the break to get in front of the fire, and then they all raced as hard as they could toward the Campbell farm.

It was dangerous. At any moment a sudden gust could have swept the fire ahead until it engulfed them. Firebrands terrified the horses. If any of the riders had been thrown, they would not have been able to get out of the way of the flames. But Louis and the others were determined. Their neighbours were at risk, and they felt they had to do everything in their power to help them.

As they raced toward the Campbell place, their horses got separated. Louis arrived at the farm before the others and took command. There was not a moment to lose.

"Turn your horses loose. They'll save themselves," he shouted in French, as the others rode in. "Jamie, let the cow out of the corral. Check and see if there are any chickens and let them go."

Campbell was stunned to see the Métis and the members of the Bains family arrive to help them save the farm. Louis ignored him. He positioned the men along the perimeter of the garden and one near the stable. He sent his brother, Joseph, along with Robbie, up on top of the house.

"What do you want me to do?" Campbell asked, uncertain of what to do next.

"You'll save your family farm," said Louis with a smile. "I want you in front with me to meet the fire."

Campbell had ploughed a fireguard to protect the garden, but it was not nearly wide enough. There was lots of water even though it had to be pumped up out of the well. As they waited for the approaching fire, the firefighters soaked the firebreak and as much of the garden as possible. They even soaked their own clothes.

The fire came in with a roar. Four big stacks of hay, which Campbell had made for his animals, were close by on the prairie. They went up with a whoosh, sending firebrands high up into the sky. It was a scramble to put them out. Campbell's stable almost caught fire, but the Métis positioned on the roof, managed to put out the blaze that began in the sod.

All along the perimeter they beat at the blaze, fighting to bring the fire under control. At one point the flames swept across the wagon road and caught in the grass near the house. Ruby was shouting as she and the children beat at the fire. Louis and Kate came running. All of them pounded at the flames with their burlap bags until their arms and shoulders ached from the effort, but they managed to stamp it out.

Jamie was in the thick of it. He fought the fire alongside Campbell, beating at the small blazes that sprung up everywhere. This time the wall of flames from the fire came so close that they could barely stand the intense heat, but they knew they had to face it or the fire would leap the firebreak, and everything would be lost. The heat was blistering. Jamie plunged his hands into the water barrel and splashed water over his face. Then he went back to fight the fire again.

They fought themselves to the point of exhaustion, and just at the time when Jamie felt he could not carry on any longer, the flames seemed to slow and then sink rapidly. The heat went out of the air and the smoke lifted. Somewhere far off the boy heard a cheer. The fire swept on past them. They had saved the farm.

Jamie walked through the garden until he found his sister Kate. Robbie was climbing down from the roof of the house. The three of them were safe. The boy felt an enormous sense of relief. He sunk to his knees on the grass outside Campbell's house, closed his eyes, and tried to rest.

Jamie looked up as he heard Ruby and Campbell talking. "You've done wrong, and you've just got to admit it," Ruby was saying.

The group of people who had come to help fight the fire were sitting out on the lawn of the Campbell place, resting and recovering from their intense battle with the prairie fire.

"You're right, Ruby, but ..." Campbell replied, looking very sheepish.

"Go ahead." Ruby had folded her arms over her generous body and stared at her husband stubbornly. "This fire showed that the Métis are true neighbours. I'm not going to leave here until you thank them," she said.

"I can't do that, Ruby. You know I don't speak the language." He was almost pleading with her.

"May I help?" asked Kate with a smile.

"There's your answer. Now I'm waitin'."

"Well, Kate. Ah ... like ... I don't know what to say." Campbell glanced at his wife, hoping she might help, but she stood, arms folded, waiting for him to make his apologies. "Maybe I should talk to Louis and Monsieur Dauphin at the same time."

"Come on then," said Kate. "Let's go over and talk to them."

She led the reluctant farmer over to where Dauphin and Louis were sitting. Campbell stood awkwardly, his hands in the pockets of his filthy work pants, his face streaked with black soot.

Dauphin looked up. *"Oui, Monsieur Campbell?"*

"Well ... Kate, would you tell Louis and Dauphin that I'm most appreciative of all the help. I would have lost the farm for sure if you Métis didn't help. And ... and, I'm real sorry for all the trouble that I caused."

Kate translated this in a blur of words and then looked back at Campbell for more.

"And ... I especially feel bad about Louis. Tell him that I'm going to see to it that all the charges and warrants against him will be cancelled. Would you say that please."

By the time that Kate had finished the translation, all the Métis were smiling. Campbell glanced up and saw Ruby nodding in encouragement. "I'm real sorry. That's all I can say. Real sorry."

Dauphin and Louis both got to their feet. They were beaming broadly. Dauphin shook the farmer's hand warmly and said, "Welcome to the neighbourhood, Campbell. *Bienvenue!*"

# 18

The fire had swept past the farms right to the brow of the hill that led down the Assiniboine River. There, the wind lifted to rise over the trees, the fire stalled and slowly burned out. The Métis farms along the river were safe.

After the great fire, Louis visited Meg every day. He would arrive after supper, and the couple would take long walks, or ride ponies far out onto the prairie, where they talked endlessly under the stars. About a week later, Louis asked if he could talk to the family.

"Meg has said that I must talk to everyone," the Métis explained with a shy smile. "She says that the Bains family always decide things together."

"Indeed that is the case," Peggy confirmed, laughing.

It was a warm August evening, and the family members were sitting around the fire pit preparing their supper after another day of hard work. The sun was beginning to set with a spectacular display of gold and red.

Louis started slowly speaking in English. "To the west of us is the Saskatchewan Territory. It is a new country of prairie lands where the Métis people are free to live as they choose. This summer I rode to a settlement called Batoche on the North Saskatchewan River. I chose a strip of land going back from the river for a farm, and I started to build a house upon it."

Louis paused for a moment, trying to gauge the reaction of his audience. "I have asked Meg if she will marry me and go to Batoche and live the life of a Métis with me," he continued. "She has agreed but would like to go with your blessing." He had finished his speech and looked up, not knowing what to expect.

"Married?" said Kate, as an excited smile spread across her face.

Meg felt very uneasy about the prospect of leaving her family. "Yes, a married woman," she answered shyly.

"But that means you will go away," Robbie added.

"I'll write, and you can come and visit," Meg said, looking anxiously at the other members of her family. "What do you think, Mother?"

Peggy smiled and said, "I could tell that this was coming, but I just worry that you are so young."

"No younger than you were when you got married."

"Well, that is true."

"And you, Jamie?" Meg asked.

A soft smile came over her brother's face. "We've been together a long time, Meg. I am going to miss you a whole lot. But I know that this will make you happy."

Jamie got to his feet and shook Louis' hand enthusiastically and then hugged his sister. All of the other members of the Bains family joined in, laughing and hugging each other in one great warm embrace.

"When's this marriage going to happen?" Kate asked above the ruckus.

"Not before the harvest. That's all I demand," said their mother, laughing. "Not before the harvest."

That night, the date of the wedding was set for mid-October. It was hard to forget about an impending event of such importance, but their mother insisted that they spend all of their time working on the harvest over the next few weeks.

They had lost about an acre of wheat with the fire, but the rest was slowly ripening. Peggy was still worried. A heavy rain or hail, coming late in the season, could beat the wheat into the ground and destroy the crop. What if the temperature dropped, and the wheat froze before they could get it out of the field? But most of all she worried about the work. Could the family get everything accomplished before winter set in? And there was one final nagging question: would they get a good price when they took the grain to the mill?

Two days after the announcement of the wedding, Campbell rode in and talked with Peggy over a cup of tea. "You sure have proven me wrong, Mrs. Bains," he commented. "I really didn't think wheat would ripen in the short growing season on the prairies. You're a better farmer than any of the rest of us."

Peggy smiled proudly. "Red Fife — it's the best wheat in the world. It will transform this country."

But as they chatted Peggy explained her concerns about the harvest. "We don't even have the right tools. We'll have to cut the wheat with that little sickle of ours."

"Now, don't you worry about nothin'" said Campbell reassuringly.

"But we need to start the harvest tomorrow and ..."

"Neighbours are here to help. That's the least we can do after the help you and your family have given us."

Everyone was told that the next day they were to start the harvest, and they were to be prepared to work nonstop until it was completed. Before sunrise the family was up and dressed. Louis arrived in his heavy work clothes. No sooner had the sun broken the horizon of a beautiful early fall day than they saw the whole Campbell family arriving on a big wagon pulled by their workhorse. In the back of the wagon was the most important tool of all: the big, long-handled scythe used for cutting hay and grain.

Ruby was talking even before the wagon had reined in. "Isn't it a fine day for a harvest?" The smile of the big woman radiated from her round, rosy face. She was wearing a dark cotton dress, sunbonnet, and snowy white apron. "Now,

Jamie, you take that big iron cauldron and set it up over that there fire," she said. "Robbie, you bring the sack of flour. I'm gonna cook up a feed for the harvestin' crew like you've never seen before in yer life."

In no time the boys had unloaded a pile of things from the wagon and set up a table under the big tree down by the stream. Soon she had the fire stoked up and was beginning to prepare mounds of food.

"Now go and attack that field of wheat," she ordered the boys. "Be back here at noon, and I'll have a nice hot lunch for everyone."

The sun was already baking the land as the harvesters gathered at the edge of the wheat field. Campbell leaned up against his long scythe and said, "Well, there's never been a harvest without the shedding of a little sweat. Let's get at it."

Peggy was dressed in her heavy farm work clothes. "If you can start the mowing, Campbell, the rest of us will come behind. Louis, Kate, and Jamie can tie the bundles into sheaths, and Meg, Robbie, and I will stook."

Campbell was good at his job. Each cut of the big blade deposited a wide swath of wheat on the ground. Soon the farmer's heavy blue work shirt and overalls were soaked with sweat, but he moved along the field without a pause, one stroke after another of the big scythe, until he got to the end. Then he turned around and came back, cutting every step of the way.

Behind him, Louis, Jamie, and Kate gathered up the wheat into sheaths and tied them with a strong cord. They chased after every stock of wheat, not missing one.

"I'm dying of thirst," Kate complained as they got to the end of the field.

"Go and get a bucket of water for everyone," suggested her older brother, "But come right back. We've got to keep up to the mowing."

She took off at a dead run and struggled back with a brimming metal bucket and tin cups. Everyone took a break, but not for long. "It's already, mid-morning," said Peggy. "We've got to push on if we want to finish by nightfall."

Hoards of grasshoppers leapt out of the way as the stookers gathered up the bundles into stooks and stood them up for drying. It was dusty work. Their faces soon darkened with the dirt.

"My back's stiff," Robbie complained.

"Better to have a stiff back now than a hungry belly in January," was his mother's only reply.

Peggy was not about to listen to petty complaints. She knew that the harvest was the most important thing in the life of the farm, and nothing — not objections from her children, blisters, dust, or heat — would stop her now.

There was a rhythm to the work. When Campbell got tired, he turned the scythe over to Louis, and when he grew tired, Jamie took a turn. Meg, Robbie, and Peggy did the stooking and then traded off with others to gather and tie up the bundles.

In the late morning, Frank and Albert rode in on their big horses. "We heard there was a harvestin' bee goin' on," said Frank with a big smile. The others welcomed him, and he pitched in, taking a turn on the scythe as if he enjoyed the chance to work.

Albert was reluctant at first. He held back from the crowd and looked awkward. Peggy joked with him, trying to make him feel at ease. "Come on, Albert. We'll have no layabouts here. Give me a hand with the stooking." Once the farmer had a job, he seemed more relaxed and worked nonstop with the others.

It was midday, and more than half the field was cut, tied and stooked, when they heard a pot ringing over by the campfire announcing lunch. The entire crew dropped its tools and headed over in a rush.

Ruby stood in front of the long table filled with food, her face beaming with good spirits. There were big, steaming bowls of delicious stew and fresh white bread baked in the Campbell oven that very morning. Jugs of frothy milk were served along with hot tea.

"There's nothin' more important than a big feed," the ample woman declared. "Come and have a good tuck-in." After everyone was seated, she plunked herself down on one of the makeshift benches and watched with pleasure as the ravenous harvest crew attacked the meal like starving animals.

Ruby was serving big slices of cornmeal cake, cooked in a frying pan over the open fire, when Dauphin and his son Joseph rode in. Campbell got up and held Dauphins' horse as he climbed down. They shook hands warmly.

"Looks like most of the work is done," Dauphin said in French. Kate translated for the others.

"We'll save you some. Don't worry," Campbell replied. The two men sat together, friends at last.

As they were finishing lunch, Peggy seized the opportunity that she had been looking for. "Ruby, look at all these young people here," she said. "Don't you think we need a school?"

"Absolutely Peggy, and we're gonna have one, too."

There was a collective moan from all the kids, but Peggy ignored them. "What do you think, Monsieur Dauphin?" she asked in French. "Will you send your children if we set up a school?"

The Métis smiled and said, "The fire showed we could work and live together. I don't know about the others, but I'll send my children to your school."

Peggy beamed. "We'll have fifteen children. That will be enough to get money for the school."

By the end of the day, they had finished cutting, tying, and stooking the entire wheat field. As they headed home, the harvesters were all exhausted but satisfied at a good day's work.

This was just the beginning of the hard work of the harvest. The day after they had finished mowing and stooking the wheat field, the members of the Bains family turned their efforts to taking in the crop from the garden. Jamie and Kate dug potatoes and carrots until they thought they could not stand it anymore while the others picked the beans, peas, and other crops that grew on vines. Carefully, Peggy stored the vegetables in wooden boxes and put them in the root cellar that they had dug close to the house. At least the family would eat well that winter.

On the evening of the third day after the harvest, Peggy came back from the fields with an announcement. "The wheat is dry enough. We'll start threshing tomorrow."

"I've got the flail made," said Jamie. "I just hope it works.

Early the next morning the family went into the wheat field. First Meg and Peggy spread the canvas that they had used as a lean-to on the ground and lay wheat sheaves on the canvas.

"All right, Jamie. Pound it with your flail," his mother said.

The flail was made from two sticks fastened loosely together at one end with a leather thong. He whipped one of the sticks in the air, and the other came down with such force that it knocked the grains of wheat off the stocks. The kernels were then scooped up by hand and put into bags.

Over and over again, Jamie whipped his flail over his head and pounded the wheat as hard as he could. In half an hour blisters were beginning to rise on his hands, and he was covered in sweat, and in an hour he was bushed. "You try," he said, handing the flail to Meg.

"Your hands are a mess, Jamie." His mother was concerned.

"They'll be all right," he replied. The boy knew that the harvest was important, and he was determined to do his part no matter what his aches and pains.

The threshing of the grain went on all that day until sundown and continued the next day. Jamie would work at it as long as he could. Then Meg would take a turn, followed by Peggy and every other member of the family. Louis and his younger brother Joseph, came to help, but still the work progressed slowly.

Finally, after three full days of work, the threshing was finished. Everyone was exhausted by the effort, but they had almost two hundred bushels of wheat ready to haul to the flour mill in Portage la Prairie. The yield was forty bushels to the acre. Peggy was overjoyed with the harvest, but the real question was, Would they get a good price?

Monsieur Dauphin had lent them some burlap bags, which they filled with the kernels of wheat. The day after they completed the threshing, they stacked as many bags filled with grain into the Red River cart as they could manage, hitched Baby to the yoke, and Peggy, Jamie, Kate, and Robbie set off. Meg stayed behind with Louis to finish bringing in the crops from the garden.

Baby lumbered slowly across the prairie toward the trail that led to the ford over the Assiniboine. The Red River cart squealed as the axle turned. The land, still blackened from the fire, was beginning to send up new shoots of grass and brush. The fall gave a nip in the air. Soon snow would cover the vast prairie landscape. They had brought in the harvest just in time.

Jamie braked the heavy cart all the way down the hill to ease the heavy load for Baby. At the ford they found the river so shallow that the water was barely up to their knees. Another mile and the cart, with the family walking beside it, was rolling down the main street of town.

Only Peggy had gone to the trouble of putting on good clothes. The others had on the rough and worn clothing that they had been wearing since they arrived at their farm. As they walked past the shop buildings, they became very conscious of the way they looked. It felt strange to be in town again after months of living on their homestead out on the bald prairie.

"Civilization at last," Kate commented.

"What makes you think towns and cities are civilized?" Robbie asked seriously. The others laughed. The young boy truly loved the wide open spaces and could not have cared less what people thought of his appearance.

Portage la Prairie had a new grist mill, and they drove the cart there without stopping. Peggy felt very nervous. "Wait with the cart," she said to the other members of the family.

"Why can't we come inside?" asked Robbie.

"Everything depends on getting a good price for our grain," was all she would say. Then she disappeared inside the office of the grist mill.

For the longest time, they waited out in the dusty street. Women, dressed in town finery, walked by staring at their scruffy, worn clothing. A gang of young kids came along and taunted them by asking if they were lost. Jamie scowled, and they scampered out of sight, laughing.

Finally their mother came out with a serious-looking bearded man wearing a bowler hat and a business suit. They were talking intently about the quality of grain and the price it would bring in places like Toronto and Montreal. The man opened each bag, took out handfuls of the wheat and let it sift through his fingers. Then, as quickly as he appeared, he disappeared back into the office with Peggy following behind.

They waited a long time again. First Robbie and then the others climbed up on the sacks of grain. Passing townspeople eyed them suspiciously. Jamie was just beginning to get worried when their mother suddenly appeared. She was beaming.

"It's perfect," she said to her children, excitement getting the better of her. "Wonderful! They bought all of our wheat. And for a good price. Red Fife — that's what they want. It will be part of the first shipment of Manitoba wheat to Ontario."

What a celebration. The mill had advanced cash in part payment, and the four of them went to the best hotel in town. The innkeeper stared at their rough clothing disdainfully, but Peggy only smiled and led her brood of children to a large square table that was covered with a white linen tablecloth and sterling silver.

The black-suited waiter, with a white cloth over his arm, addressed them formally: "Yes, madam. How may we help you?"

Peggy did not even look at the menu. "We'll have roast beef and potatoes and gravy — yes, lots of gravy." She closed her eyes, imagining the wonder of restaurant food. "And pie." She looked at the others and laughed. "Big thick pieces of pie."

"Apple!" beamed Robbie. "I want apple pie, please."

"You shall have it, young man," replied the waiter, catching the excitement of the occasion. And they ate until they felt completely stuffed.

Before they left town, they went to the hardware store and spent an hour buying a brand-new wood stove. The one they finally chose had a big oven and fire box with beautiful lettering moulded on the oven door saying, "Manitoba, Canada."

"From now on we're going to eat proper meals," their mother told them as they rolled out of town.

It took five trips on each of the next five days before they had hauled all of the wheat to the flour mill in their Red River cart. By the time they had finished, Peggy had opened a bank account and had money in it. The members of the Bains family were beginning to feel like they were finally established.

With this new sense of security, Peggy set out to buy some of the things they needed. On the second trip into town, Meg came with them. The entire family went to a store and bought enough cloth to make new clothes for everyone. Meg chose fine white muslin material for her wedding dress. At the lumber mill, they ordered planks to put a floor in their sod hut and bought two windows and a door. They bought a saw, hammer, nails, pots and pans, soap, dishes, and two kerosene lamps. At the end of the buying spree, their mother had a special gift for the three youngest members of the family: a new saddle for the mare. Now they could ride in style.

The day after, Ruby came to town with them, and the two women went off to interview the prospective teacher. Afterward, over lunch, Ruby and Peggy talked for a long time about the location of the new schoolhouse, the teacher's salary, books, and budgets.

Once the grain was delivered, the family turned its efforts to the preparation for the wedding. Everyone had to have a new outfit, and the family was organized into teams of sewers who made new shirts, trousers, and skirts for the big occasion. Meg and Peggy spent hours sewing the white cotton cloth into a lovely, flowing bridal gown.

The wedding feast normally took place at the bride's house, but there was no way that Peggy could organize such an event in their sod hut and do everything else for the wedding. In his usual generous manner, Dauphin offered to hold the feast and the dancing at their place down by the river.

Two weeks before the wedding, Peggy sat down with Jamie and told him that because his father was dead, and his older brother John was away, he would have to play the role of father in the wedding for Meg. Jamie had never done a thing like this, and he was more than a little nervous, but he was willing to do anything for his sister Meg.

Jamie wrote invitations in both English and French, and he and Robbie delivered them to the entire community. Louis found the priest and lined up the fiddlers for the party. This was to be a Métis wedding, and all of the Métis traditions were to be followed.

Several times Jamie met with Monsieur Dauphin to make sure that everything was going smoothly. The boy was accepted by the Métis almost as a man and with good reason. He had grown over the summer and was now two inches taller than his mother. His body was lean and strong, hardened from the summer of work. Jamie had a watchful look about him that was characteristic of those who knew how to live and survive on the prairie.

Four days before the event, the family members were in a complete panic as they rushed to get things done. Peggy and Meg worked endlessly on the wedding grown. Ruby came over for two days to help finish the sewing and baking. She brought her usual good-natured enthusiasm. Soon she was baking things in the oven of the new stove, sewing clothes for Jamie, Kate, and Robbie and organizing her husband to run errands. The three youngest in the Bains family made several trips down to the Dauphin place to bring the fresh-baked food and carry messages. It seemed like there was no end to the little details.

On the morning of the wedding, everyone was up early to wash and get dressed. Jamie had arranged to borrow Campbell's new buckboard and had trained the buffalo pony to pull it. As the time approached, the boy got dressed in his new suit and hitched up the rig.

Meg emerged from the sod hut in her long white gown like a princess out of a fairy tale. She looked beautiful. Her blond hair was swept back from her face and adorned with a crown of prairie flowers. Her radiant smile showed how happy she was. In that rough homestead, out on the edge of the frontier, she had been transformed from a hard-working farm girl into an exquisite beauty.

The whole family rode across the prairie in the buckboard. They picked up the river road and followed it to the Dauphin place. When they arrived they found two hundred guests — Métis and English alike — gathered in the clearing for the wedding.

Meg and Louis were married under the trees down by the river. Jamie stood beside his sister and gave away the bride. There was not a dry eye among the members of the Bains family by the time the ceremony was ended.

Following Métis tradition a huge ox was roasted over a big fire pit. Long tables were laden with potatoes and vegetables of all kind. There were pots of beans and fresh-baked bread, saskatoon berry pies, and plum puddings. People ate until they were completely full.

As the evening gathered, the party began. Four fiddlers assembled in the house, and they took turns playing fast jigs and reels without stopping. As soon as the music started, the dancing began. A Métis man, dressed in a shirt, trousers, a long red sash, and moccasins, would jump to his feet. A woman, in her long colourful gown, would face him. The two would dance intricate steps, bouncing to the rhythm of the fiddles as fast and as hard as they could until one of them was

completely exhausted and had to drop out. Immediately another person would take his or her place. The audience joined
in with shouts of encouragement to the dancers and lively
dance steps of their own.

Everyone had a turn. The Campbells danced a jig to the
loud applause of the Métis. Frank had his eye on a pretty
Métis girl, and the two got up to dance a lively reel. Even
Albert was coaxed out onto the dance floor by a dark-eyed
beauty in a blue dress.

Kate was watching the dancing in awe when Louis'
younger brother, Joseph, asked her to dance with him. The
girl could feel her face turn an embarrassing deep red, but she
soon was dancing to the fast rhythm of the fiddles. Over the
summer Kate had changed from a young girl into a strong,
independent, and very pretty young woman.

Late in the evening Peggy was standing outside, enjoying
the cool evening air and listening to the music when Dauphin
came up. He sighed and looking up at the stars he said in
French, "It has been a wonderful wedding."

"Thanks to you, Dauphin. We are much in your debt for
the help you have given us over the last few months."

"You are too modest, Peggy. You and your family have
accomplished everything yourself. You are much admired in
the Métis community." He laughed. "Maybe we should find
you a good buffalo hunter for a husband."

She smiled and said, "I think not. I am content with the
life I have."

Dauphin turned serious and added, "I fear that the life of
the Métis is changing and will never be the same. The buffalo
have gone. English settlers like yourself are farming on the
open prairie. Soon the Métis will vanish from this place, and
it will be like we were never here."

Peggy searched for something to say to console him. "The Métis will always be a part of the spirit of Manitoba," she answered softly.

The dancing went on all night without stop. Meg and Louis slipped away at some point. At dawn they arrived outside the Dauphin place with their Red River cart fully loaded and pulled by a massive ox. They were ready for their trip west to the Saskatchewan Territory. Final goodbyes were said, and the couple disappeared along the trail accompanied by the squeaking of the cart wheels.

It was over but just beginning. The next week school started for the children. Three weeks later, on a day when the taste of winter was in the air, Jamie, Kate, and Robbie were riding home from school on their ponies when they saw a man carrying a large bundle. He was a long distance away, but he was walking toward their sod hut.

It was unusual for a solitary man to be walking out on the prairie so far away from any settlement. Jamie reined in his horse and watched.

The man came steadily closer. There could be no doubt now. He had to be heading to their place. The boy urged his horse into an easy trot and rode toward him. Then suddenly he was in a full gallop and was shouting to the others.

"It's John! Ride and tell Mother! It's our brother John! He's home at last!"